The Poet and the Castle

Conisbrough Castle, Volume 7

Christopher Webster

Published by Christopher Webster, 2020.

This is a work of fiction. Similarities to real people, places, or events are entirely coincidental.

THE POET AND THE CASTLE

First edition. April 20, 2020.

Copyright © 2020 Christopher Webster.

ISBN: 979-8223542735

Written by Christopher Webster.

Table of Contents

INTRODUCTION 1

PART 1 | | "Noli Me Tangere" | I 2

II 9

III 12

IV 19

V 26

PART 2 | "The bell tower showed me such a sight..." | I .. 34

II 43

III 46

IV 55

V 59

PART 3 | "Such hap as I am happed in..." | I 66

II 73

III 82

IV 89

V 92

VI 99

VII 104

VIII 110

IX 115

PART 4: | "And I myself, myself always to hate." | I 121

II 124

III 130

AFTERWORD 139

HISTORICAL NOTE 141

BIBLIOGRAPHY 145

INTRODUCTION

Conisbrough Castle has always played a central role in English history, and is linked with a glittering array of kings, crusaders and knights, yet in the 1530's it was associated with another man who was famous for a very different reason—Thomas Wyatt, the poet (1503-1542). Wyatt was made Constable of Conisbrough Castle in 1536, and soon after, found himself having to hold the castle against the army of the Pilgrimage of Grace. Unfortunately for Wyatt, the army consisted of over 40,000 men. Most of the main events in my story actually happened, though Conisbrough Castle was never invested by the Pilgrims. However, it was provided with a large garrison and artillery as a precaution, and there can be little doubt that its threatening presence played a part in defeating the pilgrimage. This story also touches on Wyatt's love affair with Anne Boleyn, as well as the romantic aspirations of a poor gawk of a lad, a fictional character called Harry.

PART 1

"Noli Me Tangere"

I

Hugh was on guard in the lookout tower, which is the highest tower in the west curtain wall of Conisbrough Castle. It provides a commanding view of the town and directly overlooks the barbican, which in former times, allowed defenders to pour down a punishing fire on any foe who dared to attack the gatehouse. But the Wars of the Roses were over and King Henry's throne was secure. So was Hugh's, but his 'throne' was nothing more than a rickety three-legged stool which he used to ease his aching legs during his long hours on guard. His habit was to lean back against a merlon, while occasionally scanning the area below through the adjacent crenel. He was dressed as comfortably as he could get away with. Underneath his frayed and faded jupon, bearing the arms of the kingdom, for the castle was in the stewardship of the crown, was nothing more defensive than a leather jerkin. Beside him on the pavement was a sallet helmet of the simplest kind, without a visor. He had accommodated his pot-belly by slackening his sword-belt to the last notch, and as he only rarely troubled to trim his beard or cut his hair, his appearance was somewhat unkempt. None of this mattered, however, for visitors to the castle were few, and invariably came with peaceful intent.

Hugh settled himself more comfortably against the merlon, not forgetting to give the landscape a quick scan through the crenel. Then he sat up suddenly. What was that? Two horsemen heading towards the outer gatehouse – and not just any horsemen. He could tell from their rich attire and the thoroughbred horses they rode that they were gentlemen. He stood up, took a deep breath, and hauled his guts in with the belt, fastening it again on a tighter notch. Then he put on his helmet, smoothed down his jupon, and hurried down the steps to the gatehouse. Once there, he rang the bell to let the other inhabitants of the castle know that they had visitors, and picking up a halberd that was leaning against the wall, he stood to attention at the gate in his best soldierly manner.

Moments later, he was joined by a boy of about fifteen, a tall, gangling lad, who had outgrown his ragged clothes (if they had ever fitted him).

"Who is it, Mr Goodlad?" he said.

"Two gen'lefolks. Nah, mind yer manners, 'Arry, like ah've taught yer, and 'elp 'em tek their 'osses to t' stables. Tha's supposed to be 't stable lad after all!"

Soon after, an elderly man joined the small welcoming committee. He also was wearing a jupon bearing the arms of the kingdom, but it was of much better quality and in much newer condition. Below it could be seen his black hose and court shoes. He was wearing a Venetian cap of red felt, which had the effect of emphasising the greyness of his hair and beard, both of which were thin and straggly. His frame was tall and spare, though with a slight stoop – the result of age, for it was a few years since he had celebrated his sixtieth birthday. Nevertheless his blue eyes were sharp, and gave the impression that he knew everything that was going on – and a lot more besides. Around his waist was a leather belt. From the right side hung a small dagger, and from the left a huge bunch of keys, the symbol of his office as seneschal.

"What is it, Hugh?" he asked mildly.

"Two gen'lemen, sir," answered the man-at-arms.

Moments later, the two gentlemen were at the gate, probably wondering why they had not been challenged at the ruinous gate of the outer bailey, or the crumbling gate of the barbican.

Hugh barred their way, as was his duty, and asked their business, but before either of them could reply, the old man was bidding them welcome.

"Well, if it isn't young Thomas!" he said. "I am very glad to see you. How's your father?"

The man whom he had called "young Thomas" was well into middle age, as could be seen from his grizzled beard. He sat tall in the saddle, and as he stepped down from his horse, his true size – over six feet – became apparent. He held himself in a proud and confident manner, as befitted the son of a wealthy landowner.

"I'm not 'young Thomas', any more, Melton. There's another 'young Thomas' now, and here he is."

The other man, who had also dismounted, made a bow to the old gentleman.

Wyatt said, introducing them, "Meet Thomas Wyatt, my son – only fifteen, but nearly as big as me. I'm taking him around with me as a sort of squire. I want to prepare him for his first appointment at court. Tom, this is John Melton, Esquire, seneschal of the castle."

"Well, how the years do fly!" said Melton to Wyatt. "It seems like only yesterday that your father was showing *you* the ropes. How is he, by the way?"

"79 and still healthy, thanks be to God. He resigned his post as Treasurer of the King's Chamber and the Royal Mint a few years ago, but he still keeps his constableships – though this one is too far for him to travel to, these days. That's why I'm here."

"I'm delighted to see you, and your business won't take long. There's little enough to see here. We can go over the books tomorrow – but I'm keeping you here talking and you must be dying of thirst! Harry, tell Sally to put out some cold meats, bread and ale. Then she can air the bedchamber and make up the beds.

The seneschal led the way to a range of buildings along the inside of the north curtain wall. A magnificent arched doorway led to the Great Hall, and Melton showed them to a table at the lower end, near to the kitchen. Wyatt glanced towards the high table, where he had once sat with his father at a feast many years ago. The afternoon light slanted in from four high, gothic windows, and picked out some of the painted decorations on the slender columns that supported the hammer beams of the roof. On the north wall was a huge fireplace, empty, but magnificent with its brightly painted escutcheons and its flanking tapestries depicting scenes from the life of King

Arthur. Somehow the hall, though imposing in its majesty, wore a forlorn aspect. It was clean enough, but it had that musty smell of a place that is not often used. They lingered in the hall for a moment, then the seneschal led them through a small door into the kitchen and called for food and drink.

Wyatt swilled the ale with relish. "A fine brew, this," he said.

"I prefer Allington ale," said young Tom. "This is too bitter."

Melton fired up in its defence. "That's a local ale made at the Castle Brewery, down by the brook, and better than anything they serve up down south, I'll be bound."

"It's Tom's first time in the north," said Wyatt, "but I'm glad he's got the chance to see it. The Wyatts are an old Yorkshire family, though we're settled in Kent now."

"How do you like Conisbrough?" said Melton.

The touch of pride in Melton's voice was enough to make Tom careful about his answer.

"Beautiful scenery – I mean, the river, and those white cliffs behind it. But the town looks... poor."

He was going to say "like a rubbish dump", but thought the better of it.

"I've lived here all my life," said Melton, "and it's always been poor. Finest people on earth, though, and honest as the day is long – except when it comes to paying rent. You see, the bad harvest last year has led to high food prices, and some tenants are in difficulty. But I'll explain about that when we do the ledger."

"My father still has a soft spot for the old place," said Wyatt."He often tells me stories about his time here."

Melton laughed at a sudden recollection.

"Do you remember that business with Thomas Drax?"

"I remember the name – something about cattle, wasn't it?"

"Yes, Drax was grazing his cattle on a piece of land hard by Conisbrough Common. Indeed, your father asserted that it *was* part of Conisbrough Common, and that only the people of Conisbrough had the right to graze their cattle there. Drax disputed this, and took no notice. So one night, Wyatt, with Tom Kendall and a dozen men-at-arms, armed and at midnight, to drive the cattle into the bailey here, and he kept them there till they starved – those were the days when the castle still had a garrison to be proud of!"

Wyatt laughed too.

"I remember now. I wanted to go with him, but he said I was too young. I remember those poor cattle trying to nibble the bits of grass that grew through the cobbles. I could never understand why my father didn't butcher them properly and sell the meat."

Melton shook his head.

"No, no. He was a wise man, your father, and knew the law better than most. If he had attempted to profit by it he would have been guilty of cattle stealing. As it was, he could claim it was a just punishment for the trespasser – nor did he leave it there. A few days later he went with 18 men-at-arms and seized the land in the name of Conisbrough. The local burghers were so impressed with this defence of the rights of Conisbrough folk that, at the manoral court of Conisbrough in October of that year – 1519, I think it was – how the years do fly! – he was elected Reeve of Conisbrough and Braithwell."

"He often said he preferred Conisbrough politics to affairs of state," said Wyatt.

"That's because he has the common touch."

Just then, Sally came in with another jug of ale. Though not quite fifteen, she was a well-developed girl with a pretty face and a saucy wit.

"Is there owt else yer'll be wantin', sir?" she said.

"Say 'anything'," corrected Melton. "You'll never get anywhere if you speak like that."

"No, sir. Thank you, sir," she replied, with a slight bob that passed for a courtesy.

Tom looked at her appreciatively, no doubt thinking that not everything in Conisbrough was 'rubbish'.

II

Later, Melton took them up to their private apartments. These consisted of two rooms, a bedroom and a study, both wainscotted with dark oak. Over the small fireplace was a portrait of Henry Wyatt, Thomas' father. It was nothing like the large Holbein which hung in the Great Hall at Allington Castle. That showed the statesman, serious, wealthy, with a gold chain of office around his neck. This showed a younger man in ragged clothes, a prisoner, with a cat beside him, a dead pigeon in its mouth.

"Is it true, that story about the cat?" asked Melton.

"It is," said Wyatt with a touch of family pride. "My father was imprisoned by King Richard because of his loyalty to Henry Tudor. He was tortured with a horse barnacle to make him change his loyalty, but somehow he held out – knowing my father it was pure stubbornness! Worse of all he was given no food, and nearly starved to death. However, he befriended the prison cat, Acater, and every now and then it would bring him a pigeon, which gaoler agreed to cook for him. He got his reward when Henry Tudor finally became King Henry VII."

"So he was saved by a cat?"

"He was," said Thomas, "but he always points out that the important thing was loyalty. It was his undying loyalty that made him the man he is now – hence his motto: *loyaulte me lie* – loyalty binds me."

"A good example for his sons."

"I hope so," said Wyatt. "I am loyal to King Henry, but, heaven knows – he makes it difficult enough sometimes."

Then, conscious, perhaps, that he had said too much, he turned the subject, "but enough of that. Show us the bedchamber."

The bedchamber was a similar wainscotted room with a small fireplace in which a fire was burning merrily. The windows had been thrown open, and the bedclothes thrown back.

Young Thomas was about to leap onto the bed to test it, when Wyatt noticed something in the middle of the bed.

"Stop!" he said. "Why, that's..."

He reached forward and picked it up. It was his father's lute – his second best lute – the best was at Allington. This was a small-bodied instrument with a back of variegated rosewood and maple, strung with six courses.

He strummed a chord and grimaced.

"Out of tune!"

"It's a long time since it was played," said Melton, "but I always keep it here to keep it dry, as your father instructed."

Wyatt sat on the bed and began to tune it.

"This is the lute I learned on," he said. Then, satisfied with the tuning, he began to play. After a few bars, he laughed, put it down, and began to recite on of his poems:

> *Blame not my Lute! for he must sound*
> *Of this or that as liketh me;*

For lack of wit the Lute is bound
To give such tunes as pleaseth me;
Though my songs be somewhat strange,
And speak such words as touch thy change...

"In other words, if the lute sounds bad, it's because of my playing. I'm getting rusty, and must make a point of practising while I am here."

Then he turned to Tom.

"Speaking of which, it's about time I taught you. A gentleman should know how to play the lute as well as how to wield a sword. Now, these are the griffs, or stops... but where is that book I learned from? It must be here, somewhere."

Melton judged this a good moment to withdraw.

"I will leave you to recreate yourselves, and will send Sally when dinner is ready. That will be at five – none of your fancy southern ways here, you know."

III

This time they dined at the high table. The seat of honour was reserved for the lord of castle, who was none other than King Henry VIII. In his absence it was left empty as a mark of respect, with Wyatt seated at its immediate right hand, and Melton to the right of him. Young Tom occupied the next seat. A fire had been lit in the great fireplace, and two cressets flared on the nearest columns. A three-branched candelabrum stood in the middle of the table. The flames flickered in the ever-present draft, and sent long shadows dancing around the hall, as though the ghosts of the long extinct De Warennes were reliving one of their great feasts. The figure of Sir Lancelot on the tapestry stirred in the draft and caught a glimmer from a flaring torch, and it seemed as though he was hurrying to join them. A flagon of Rhenish wine from Melton's dwindling cellar completed the feast, as well as the illusion.

"All we need is a lutenist," said Melton.

Wyatt thought of Smeaton and looked gloomy, but Tom failed to notice it. "And a singer – preferably a fair one," then noticing Sally, he added. "Oh, look. Here she is!"

Sally, followed by her mother, was serving a pheasant. Hugh followed, transformed by a cambric apron into a serving-man, carrying a large platter on which was a roasted sucking pig.

"It may not look much to London eyes," said Melton, "but believe me, this is the finest feast this hall has witnessed in many a long day – and glad I am of it. Now, set to with a will."

At these words, each man drew out his knife and began to cut hunks of bread and meat. For a while they ate in appreciative silence. Melton, because he had not tasted such good food for a long time, and the Wyatts because their appetites had been heightened by travel.

Of course, a gentleman should make polite conversation at the table, and not gobble his dinner like a dog, so Wyatt began with, "I see that Hugh waits at table, as well as doing guard duty."

"He is a Jack-of-all-trades," said Melton, "as are all of us here. It's not so long ago that there were 20 men-at-arms, a serjeant-at-arms, a groom and a stable boy – not to mention the kitchen staff and the maids, but now I have only Hugh and his family, and young Harry to help me. Hugh's wife is the cook, his daughter the maid, and Harry sees to the stables. It's the revenues, you see. The castle belongs to the king, as does the Honour of Conisbrough and all that pertains to it, but he allows nothing for maintenance, and nothing for the staff."

"How do you pay for them, then?"

"The castle itself has a number of dues which are owed directly, for example, Castlegardurn tax – but they are diminishing year by year. It's hard to collect tax from tenants who can hardly put a loaf on their table. That is when Hugh really earns his keep. For most of the month he has nothing much to do but keep a look out, but on the last day of the month he dresses in full armour and comes with me on my rounds – and believe me, it's necessary! Only last week he was attacked by farmer with a pitchfork – he's in the dungeon now, so if you hear groans and the rattling of chains in the middle of the night – don't worry, it's not a ghost."

"We are haunted by the past," said Wyatt absent-mindedly as though thinking of something else.

"What I was leading up to," continued Melton, "is that the accounts are... well, they are full of gaps. Believe me, I have tried to complete them – but what can you take from someone who has nothing?"

"We all have nothing in the end," said Wyatt, watching the shadows dancing in the gloom. Melton looked at him thoughtfully for a while. Then, making up his mind to speak out, said, "Forgive me, Wyatt, but you seem to be thinking of other things. I thought you came here to inspect the castle."

Wyatt seemed to be hypnotised by the dancing dark, and it was only with difficulty that he dragged his attention back to his host.

"Melton, You are an old family friend, so I will be frank. That was just an excuse. I came here to escape from court. Things are going badly there – for one of my friends in particular."

"Who? Do I know him?"

"Mark Smeaton."

"The name sounds familiar, but I can't place it."

"He is Groom of the Privy Chamber – in effect, he is Queen Anne's musician. It was I who introduced him to her, so I feel responsible for what has happened."

"What has happened?"

"I play the lute a little, and asked him to teach me after I heard him play at the Chapel Royal."

"Why did you need a teacher? You play well."

"A musician knows better. I am lucky if I can get the notes right, but Mark's touch on the lute is heavenly; it ravishes human sense. There is a painting at Hampton Court by Holbein called *The Ambassadors*. In the centre of the painting is a lute – that lute is his, for by the time it was painted he had become King Henry's court musician. Holbein, of course, is a genius, and not just with the brush. I think he predicted Mark's fate, for on that lute is a broken string."

"A broken string?"

"Yes. Let me tell you why..."

Just then, Wyatt noticed that the hall was strangely silent. Hugh, Mrs Goodlad and Sally were standing as though awaiting orders, but it seemed as though they were as eager to hear the story as Melton.

"...but it is for your ears only, Melton. Send your servants away."

"Bring another flagon of the Rhenish, Sally, then go to the kitchen with the others."

"You too, Tom," said Wyatt. "Better leave us to it."

"But father!" protested the youth, who was looking forward to a juicy morsel of court gossip.

"The less you know about all this the better – believe me."

"Yes father," said Tom, and got up to follow Sally, who had just set the wine on the table, without seeming too disappointed. Perhaps he had some other entertainment in mind.

When the door to the kitchen was heard to close, Wyatt continued. "Queen Anne is a sophisticated woman. She is educated and loves the arts, particularly music. She writes poetry that is better than mine and songs that are better than Ferrabosco's. Mark taught her to play the lute. Well, you saw me teaching Tom just now – it's a very physical process. Hands touch, fingers intertwine, the learner embraces the lute and the teacher embraces the learner. But don't misunderstand me. I believe that the queen is loyal to the king – she would be a fool not to be! The tales they tell are all lies…"

The shadows in the room had stopped their dancing, and seemed to be clustering around the table so that they would miss nothing – or perhaps it was just that the fire was dying down.

"What tales? Remember, I know nothing of court. The Conisbrough Moot is politics enough for me, believe me!"

"…that her pet name for him was Marmalade – because he was so sweet, and that he was sometimes concealed in the cupboard where night-time snacks were kept, until Anne called her waiting woman, 'Margaret! bring me a little marmalade', when he was undressed and brought in to her ready for her entertainment."

"Marmalade. I like that!"

The shadows shifted and Wyatt grimaced. "It's not funny. It is a dreadful calumny! The next story I heard is probably true, though. On Saturday before May Day the queen found Mark standing in the round window in her Chamber of Presence. She asked why he was so sad, and he said it was no matter, then she said, 'You may not look at me in that way because you are a commoner.' To which Smeaton replied, 'No, no madam, a look sufficeth me and thus fare you well.' The lady in waiting who reported this seems to have believed that Mark was declaring his love for the queen, but I think that Mark had been trying to warn her what was happening, and that the King was collecting evidence to get rid of her... but I have gone too far..."

The shadows began a mocking dance, then crowded close to the table as one of the cressets went out. Melton leaned closer, as though to ensure confidentiality, and said, "Have no fear, Thomas. You know me of old and know that I am no tell-tale; *loyaulte me lie* could be my motto, too. As for anyone else – these walls are thick, and by now Hugh will be in his cups, since the Castle Brewery pays the rent with barrels of beer – so you might as well tell me the rest of it now that you've begun."

The shadows leaned in close. The other cresset had gone out. The fire was burning low, and the last remaining candle was guttering in its socket.

"Not long afterwards, Cromwell tricked Smeaton by inviting him to dinner. Once he had him, he said 'I give you notice now that you will have to tell me the truth before you leave here, either by force or good-will.' Then he called two men of his, and asked for a knotted rope to be put round Mark's head, and twisted it with a cudgel until Mark confessed his affair. Then he asked Mark if he knew of anyone else besides himself who had relations with the queen. Mark, to escape further torture, said that he had seen Master Norris and Brereton, and swore that he knew no more. Then Cromwell wrote a letter to the King, and sent Mark to the Tower... and now it will be as Holbein prophesied."

Melton shook his head in disbelief.

"But I thought he was a painter."

"In his painting there is a half-concealed skull. It is painted in such a way that you can only see it if you look at the painting from an extreme angle."

"A skull is common enough in a painting. What do they call it – *memento mori* – a reminder of mortality?"

"True enough, but the lute, the broken string – and then the skull."

Melton sat up straight and said in a louder voice, "Thomas, I am surprised at you. You are as superstitious as an old woman! Why, this is the 16th century! We don't believe in signs and portents any more!"

Just then the candle went out and the shadows had possession of the room.

IV

In the kitchen, things were merrier. The great cooking fire had died down, but was still lively. Hugh was emptying his third tankard. His wife, Sally, with the little one, Totty on her lap, was finishing off the best meal they had had for many a long day – for was not 'a feast in the hall, a feast for all' in the words of the old saying?

"Weer's our Sally?" she said.

"Flirtin' wi' that young gen'leman, I'll be bound," said Hugh.

"Well, you'd better stop 'em afore there's trouble."

"You go."

"Ah canna go. Ah'm lookin' after Totty."

So with a grunt and a groan, Hugh put down his unfinished tankard, took up a candle, and went out of the kitchen door shouting, "Sally!"

That broke the spell in the hall. The ghostly shadows fled to the dark corners, and Melton and Wyatt rose from the table. It broke another spell, too. A female voice might have been heard coming from behind the stables, "That's me feyther, so yer can get yer 'and aht o' me bodice."

A husky voice might have been heard to reply, "Just one more kiss!"

But again, and louder, the insistent call was heard: "Sally!"

Hugh didn't see what was going on, but he guessed. Someone ran past him in the darkness, and a moment later he found his daughter. He grabbed her roughly by the arm and hauled her into the kitchen.

"Nah, then, thou brazen hussy, what hast tha been up to?"

"Nothin' dad."

"What! Wi' yer bodice 'alf open! I'll beat t' livin' daylights aht o' thee!"

"'Ee didn't get nowt dad. Ah'm not that daft."

Hugh, somewhat mollified by this reassurance, pushed her through the kitchen door and sat her down at the table. Then he began to lecture her. In the light of the candle he could see angry tears running down her cheeks, but also a stubborn pout on her lips.

"Listen 'ere, lass. That young gen'leman is no good for thee. 'Ee'll get thee up t' stick an' leave thee wi' nowt."

Hugh's good wife took up the theme: "Aye, you should be lookin' for a man who'll marry yer. Why don't you find yersen a nice man-at-arms like ah did."

"Oh aye, weer can ah find one o' them?" retorted Sally, "There's only me dad 'ere these days."

Hugh considered the point, then had a bright idea.

"Next time ah've to go to Tickhill Castle, ah'll tek thee. There's six men-at-arms theer, an' at least two on 'em are not married."

"Aye, an' they're paid more, an' all," said Mrs Goodlad, bringing up an old complaint.

"Ah, women!" said Hugh, not caring to go over the old ground that, with them all employed here, they were not so badly off at Conisbrough. He sat down, drained his tankard, then topped it up again. After all, wasn't the beer flowing freely now that they had 'gen'lemen' visitors?

Wyatt climbed the stairs to his apartments with the stub of a candle that Melton had found for him. He looked into the bedchamber, and saw that his son was asleep – or pretending to be asleep, then went into the study, sat down at the writing table and sunk his head in his hands.

He had said too much, perhaps. And yet, he had said nothing about what really troubled him, and that was Anne. Anne, beautiful, witty, well-educated – he liked to think of her as his old sweetheart, though she had always kept him at arm's length because he was married. A bright image of a long lost summer flashed across his mind. He and Anne were neighbours. It was not far to go on horseback from Allington to Hever, where he knew Anne was staying while her parents were at court. He spent many happy days there, talking, laughing, flirting, writing poetry. One day, with his heart in his mouth, he gave her a paper on which was written – not an outright declaration of love, but something very close to it:

What means this when I lie alone?
I toss. I turn, I sigh, I groan.
My bed me seems as hard as stone
What means this?
And if perchance by me there pass
She unto whom I sue for grace,
The cold blood forsaketh my face.
What means this?

But if I sit near her by
With loud voice my heart doth cry
And yet my mouth is numb and dry
What means this?

She read it quickly, folded the paper, tucked it into the bosom of her gown, and with an arch look, had said, "Sir, you shall have your reply tomorrow."

Her reply was in the form of poem:

Thomas, if I returned thy love to thee
Would'st thou still as wildly worship me?
For hearts desire what they cannot attain,
And take for granted everything they gain.

And so I beg thee, at a distance stay,
And let's be happy in a lesser way.
'Twould break my heart to give you all of mine
Only to find cruel falsity in thine!

Despite these words, the poetry had brought them closer, and on one never-to-be forgotten day at Greenwich, when her father and mother were at court, he found his way to her bedroom, closed the door, kissed her, and began to unfasten her gown. Anne did not protest, and might have gone all the way, had they not been interrupted by a noise from the room above. Anne tidied herself up and ran out of the room. After an hour she returned but the mood had been broken. He had hoped he would be able to try again another day – but that day never came. Soon after, she became the toast of the court and the king began to take an interest in her. He remembered how, even then, he had tried to win her, partly through his poetry.

To wish and want and not obtain,
To seek and sue ease of my pain,
Since all I ever do is vain
What may it avail me?

Although I strive both day and hour
Against the stream with all my power,
If fortune list yet for to lour
What my it avail me?

For in despair there is no rede.
To want of ear speech is no speed.
To linger still alive as dead
What may it avail me?

But if he had turned a blind eye to his danger, Anne had not, and wrote a reply with a clear warning:

Graven with diamonds in letters plain
There is written round my neck about:
Noli me tangere *for Ceasar's I am*
And wild for to hold though I seem tame.

In other words: *Beware! I am the king's.*

After that, he had fully realised his danger, and after much agonising, decided that his best course was to tell the king everything. After all, he had been Anne's lover before the king had showed any interest in her, and the love affair had – just – remained unconsummated.

OVERCOME WITH THE EMOTION of these memories, Wyatt picked up a quill and began to scratch on a scrap of parchment that he found in a drawer of the writing table.

What death is worse than this,
When my delight,
My weal, my joy, my bliss,
Is from my sight?
Both day and night
My life, alas, I miss:
For though I seem alive,
My heart is hence;
Thus, bootless for to strive
Out of presence
Of my defence,
Toward my death I drive.
Heartless, alas, what man
May long endure?
Alas, how live I then?
Since no recure
May me assure,
My life I well may ban.
Thus doth my torment go
In deadly dread;
Alas, who might live so,
Alive as dead,

Alive to lead
A deadly life in woe?

The stub of candle flickered and died, leaving Wyatt to grope his way to the bedchamber by the dim light of the moon which filtered through the leaded panes of the study window.

V

Early next morning, Wyatt began his tour of inspection. A good night's sleep in the deep silence of a half-empty castle had done something to restore his peace of mind, and he thought he might as well make good use of his trip by doing some useful work on behalf of his father. Accordingly, after a hearty breakfast, he accompanied Melton on a tour of the castle.

"We will begin with the keep," said Melton.

He led them up a flight of narrow stone steps, and across a small drawbridge to an iron-riveted oak door, which he opened with one of the large keys which hung from his belt.

As soon as Wyatt stepped into the building he felt the damp as a tangible presence in the air, and along with it, the musty smell of decay.

"The roof's full of holes," explained Melton. "Every time it rains the water pours through onto the floor of the solar, and that's rotted through and not safe. We won't go up there, but I'll show you the Great Chamber."

Turning to the right, he led them up a wide staircase that curved with the keep wall. Long ago, this would have served as a grand approach to the lord's principal chamber. At the top of the stairs was a wooden screen, mouldy and rotten, and beyond that, the chamber itself. It was dominated by a magnificent hooded fireplace with rusty iron firedogs in the empty grate. The back of the fireplace glistened with damp.

"The chimney was blown down in storm a few years ago," said Melton, "and now the rain comes straight down into the grate."

Wyatt looked doubtfully at the floor.

"It's safe enough for now," said Melton, noticing the direction of his glance, "but if you look at the ceiling, you will see where the water comes through from above. It'll all be rotten before long."

"But can't you…"

"The king has commanded me to send him all the revenues from the Honour of Conisbrough. I am to hold nothing back for upkeep. I am sorry to say that the days of Conisbrough Castle are over. Next time you come it will be a heap of ruins. Yet I remember a time when it was a mighty presence in the county with a garrison worthy of the name."

"The day of castles is long gone," said young Tom dismissively. "Gunpowder has seen to that."

Melton shook his head. "You never know. There's enough trouble in England today, heaven knows, and where there's trouble, there's safety behind walls."

On their way out, Wyatt heard muffled cries from somewhere down below.

"Is that your prisoner?"

"Yes. Take no notice. He kicks up a fuss every time someone comes in here. I hope Hugh has remembered to feed him."

"I'd like to take a look."

"It's not easy to get down there – just a long ladder."

"Sounds like a bit of a lark," said Tom.

"Very well, but excuse me if I don't accompany you. My old bones are not up to it."

With that, he took up one of his keys and opened a large round grating in the centre of the guardroom.

"It's not really a dungeon. It's a storeroom, but with the dungeon near the gatehouse being half full of water, it's the only place where I can put prisoners. You'll need this. There are no windows."

Melton took a cresset from its bracket and lit it with his tinder box. Tom held the cresset while his father descended, then followed himself holding the ladder in one hand and the cresset in the other.

The descent was a hazardous one because the storeroom was a high, vaulted space, twice the height of the Great Chamber, and the ladder was long, and not in the best condition, so that it bent and swayed under their weight.

They had no sooner got to the bottom when a voice cried out, "Mercy!"

Tom raised the cresset and among the barrels and crates saw a ragged figure chained to an iron ring set into the wall. Beside him was a pitcher of water and an empty platter. The air was foul from the stench from a wooden bucket which stood on the other side.

"Ah beg yer, sire," pleaded the man again, "Release me!"

Wyatt looked him up and down. Whatever he had been before, he was a wretched creature now, ragged, filthy and desperate.

"I am informed that you attacked an officer of the crown. If it is true, you will surely hang for it," answered Wyatt dispassionately.

"Ah only waved me pitchfork! Ah nivver attacked anybody!"

"That's for the court to decide."

"Ah'll get a trial then?" said the man, sounding relieved.

"Yes, and then they'll hang you."

"But ah only waved…"

"Hugh, the man-at-arms, will give his evidence, and if he tells the magistrate what he told me, then you'll hang for sure."

The prisoner let out a great howl and pulled at his chains. Then fell in a pitiful heap, sobbing his heart out.

"Don't you feel sorry for him, father?" said Tom, clearly moved by his first sight of a condemned man.

Wyatt grimaced as he remembered the events of the past months.

"Not when an innocent man has been condemned. You know whom I speak of."

"Yes. Smeaton. But this man did little enough if what he says is true."

"He threatened a man-at-arms bearing the arms of the kingdom proclaiming him to be a king's man on the king's business. What could be worse? He will hang for it, and that will be a lesson to others. I predict that my friend Melton will have a lot less trouble collecting his dues in the months to come."

With that, they left the man and began to climb the ladder, Wyatt first.

"Leave the light!" cried the prisoner.

Tom put the cresset on a wall bracket and climbed up the ladder towards the circular opening where a dim grey light filtered in from the outer door.

"Will he really hang, sir?" said Tom to Melton as they left the keep.

"He will be tried at the next county assize, and the verdict is all but certain."

"Forget him," said his father gently. "We have far greater concerns."

Melton led them down the keep steps and across the centre of the inner bailey.

"The south curtain is in a dangerous state, as you will see from outside, so I have ordered that all the buildings against it should be boarded up. Nor are the men-at-arms – Hugh, I mean – to use the wall-walk."

Melton led them through the gatehouse where Hugh was on guard, looking more soldierly than the day before, as he had tidied his hair and beard, and put on a few extra pieces of armour. He varied turns at the gatehouse with turns on the top of the lookout tower, and walks along the northern wall-walk.

"The barbican gatehouse is in a sorry state and we daren't raise the drawbridge in case it falls to pieces. As for the outer bailey, we abandoned it years ago. The walls are partly collapsed and the gatehouse is long gone – the locals take the stone for building materials, you see. But, come this way; my main concern is the south curtain."

Melton led them along the outer bank of the castle ditch and stopped opposite the central bastion.

"Look at those cracks," he said. "Last year you could put your fingers in them. This year, it's your fist. Next year, the whole of the south curtain will be in the ditch."

Wyatt scanned the wall, and sure enough lines of jagged cracks radiated from each side of the tower.

"What's the problem? Can anything be done about it?"

"Most of the castle is built on solid rock, but there's only soil under those walls. They were undermined in a siege centuries ago and never properly repaired. Also, one tower is not enough to support them. There should be two at least. But it would cost a fortune to put it right. It's a much bigger job than re-roofing the keep."

They carried on walking, following a narrow path that led along the outer bank. As they turned north, Wyatt noticed something else that needed attention.

"Those woods..."

"That's the Castle Woods."

"Well, they should be cleared if the castle is to have any defensive value. Not that I would like to scale that escarpment. The castle must have been practically invulnerable from this side!"

Melton laughed.

"That's a little investment of mine. I planted those trees many a long year ago, and when they grow to maturity they'll be worth a fair bit. But not a word mind..."

He tapped the side of his nose confidentially.

"I'm sure my father approved."

"He did."

"Then my report will make no mention of it."

Wyatt turned to his son.

"Sometimes you have to turn a blind eye to things. It's all a matter of judgement."

"What about the prisoner?" said Tom.

"And some things you ignore at your peril."

"He's right," said Melton. "I'm a mild enough man, but I know that if I treated him leniently, I would have trouble every time I went out to collect my dues – and it's hard enough as it is.

They walked on for a while in silence, then as they turned to walk back to the barbican gatehouse parallel to the west wall, Wyatt said, "You two carry on, and I'll walk back the other way."

Perhaps it was the poet's impulse to be alone, or perhaps he wanted more private time to ponder on his problems. Whatever his original motive, he was, for a while, soothed by the beauty of the scenery. The walk back, with the Castle Woods on one side, and the overgrown escarpment on the other was more of a landscape for artists, poets and lovers than a military arena.

On an impulse, he struck out to the left of the pathway, and scrambled down the far side of the escarpment into the depths of the castle woods. Then, crossing a rough road that led to Strafford Ford, he descended another bank to the where the brook had been dammed for the mill race of Castle Mill. The tinkling of the water, and the turning of wheel were hypnotic, and transported Wyatt from the troubled scene of court life that continued to disturb his peace. As he sat a poem took shape in his mind:

From these high hills as when a spring doth fall,

It trilleth down with still and subtle course;
Of this and that it gathers aye and shall,
Till it have just off flowed the stream and force;
Then at the foot it rageth over all:
So fareth love when he hath ta'en a source;
His rein is rage, resistance Vaileth none;
The first eschew is remedy alone.

Wyatt wrote down the poem when he got back to the castle, and after another meal in the shadowy Great Hall, slept more soundly than he had done for years. He slept late next morning, for the peace was like a drug, and he felt he could live for ever in that crumbling old castle that was slowly returning to nature. But he knew he had to face the trials and traumas of King Henry's court, and that if he didn't screw up his courage and go back that very day, he might never do it at all.

A letter arrived the following morning that made his return a matter of urgency. It was from his father. Old and bedbound as he was, he was alert enough to see the dangers that faced his son. The letter urged Wyatt to get into the king's presence at once and stay there night and day, as this was the only way he could scotch the rumours that surrounded him and the queen.

PART 2

"The bell tower showed me such a sight..."

I

Wyatt wasted no time in getting ready. Melton was surprised at his haste and wondered if he had done anything to upset his guest. Wyatt replied reassuringly, "Believe me, Melton," he said, "I had a thousand times rather stay in this castle with you than dance attendance on the king. Here, the troubles are in the past; passions of love, hate and ambition have played a thousand dramatic scenes within these walls – you can sense it – you can almost see those scenes replayed in the shadows of the firelight."

Melton laughed.

"That is the poet speaking! I only see the decay and worry about it falling down."

"What I mean is," Wyatt continued. "That the love, hate and ambition are only ghosts in this castle, but at court they are in the here and now, and likely to do for me if I don't turn up to defend myself – but I have said enough. Words are as dangerous as daggers, these days."

"I understand," said Melton, "and I wish you well in the trials you will face."

"Trials," murmured Wyatt. "I don't care for that word!"

"I meant..."

"I'm sorry, old friend, but my mind is troubled and I seem to see danger in everything. Well, I must go. Where is that boy? – Tom!"

Wyatt looked scanned the inner Bailey. Mrs Goodlad and Peter were outside the kitchen, but he was not with them. Hugh could be seen on the gatehouse tower, but he was not there, either.

"Tom!" shouted Wyatt again in a louder voice.

A moment later Tom could be seen hurrying from that dark corner behind the north buttress, making it easy to guess where Sally was – though there was no sign of her, as she was, no doubt, keeping out of sight.

"Tom, get ready. We leave for London within the hour."

"But..."

Wyatt held up his letter.

"An urgent message from my father – no, don't ask. Just hurry up."

Tom looked disappointed. His explorations into the mysteries of Sally's bodice had been delightful and he had hoped to progress to the mysteries of her voluminous skirts.

THE TOWER OF LONDON was as different to Conisbrough Castle as a mountain to a mole hill, and the difference in its garrison was even greater. Instead of poor old, down-at-heel Hugh, there were so many men-at-arms that it looked as though the castle was on a war footing – which it was, in a way; King Henry's war against the church. Wyatt and his son had to thread their way though an outer gatehouse, a barbican and the Lion Tower gatehouse, and at each step they were challenged by stony faced guards.

Wyatt and Tom made his way to the White House where they had been told they might find the king, who had come down for the day from Hampton Court to see his First Minister, Thomas Cromwell. They were stopped again at the door, this time by heavyweight versions of the guards at the Lion Gate. They were both wearing full plate armour and had mean expressions on what could be seen of their faces through the barred visors of their helmets. Nothing Wyatt could say could persuade them to let him pass. He told them that he was a Gentleman of the King's Privy Chamber, that he was on urgent business, that the king was expecting him, but it made no impression. At last, seeing that he would not go away, one of them went inside to enquire from his senior officer.

He was gone for along time, but when he did finally reappear, Thomas Cromwell was close behind him. Cromwell was a man of middle height with a slightly plump face and slight double chin that would have given him the appearance of a comfortable burgher were it not for the look of steely determination in his eyes, and the firm line of his unsmiling lips.

"Ah! Essex! I am glad to see you," Wyatt began. "Now, will you tell these oafs to let me pass. I must see the king."

But Cromwell did not respond to his friendly greeting. Instead, he shook his head and frowned.

"I'm sorry, Wyatt, but you cannot see the king."

Wyatt made as if to protest, but Cromwell cut him off.

"Perhaps you have heard. There are investigations under way. Indeed, your name has been mentioned somewhat."

The blood drained from Wyatt's face. He was too late! His enemies had got to the king first, and now he would have no chance to plead his case in person.

"In that case..." said Wyatt, and turned to go.

"Wait," said Cromwell. "You cannot leave. You are needed as a witness."

Wyatt took a step away from the door. A guard immediately walked around him to cut off his retreat.

Cromwell gave a rather false laugh.

"Don't misunderstand me, Wyatt. You are not under arrest – but you must stay here in the Tower at the King's convenience."

Wyatt wanted to say, "If I am not free to go, then I am, in effect, under arrest," but the poet in him knew the power of words, and knew that Cromwell was attempting to gloss over an unpleasant reality. He also knew that his best tactic was to go along with it.

"Very well," he said, "I am always ready to be of service to my king."

Cromwell gave a thin smile and a slight nod, as if to say, "Very wise, for if you had attempted to resist you would have found yourself in the dungeon." Instead, he said, "You can stay in the Upper Bell Tower. You will find that is well appointed. There is a private chamber, a bed chamber and a garderobe."

Wyatt grimaced at the thought. Well appointed or not, it was still a prison. He turned to Tom, who had been watching this interchange with disbelief, and said, "Tom, go to Allington and tell your grandfather what has happened."

He said no more because he didn't want Cromwell to hear his plans – though 'hopes' would be a more accurate word. His father still had great influence in court, and he hoped he might be able to use it to set him free. In the meantime, he had no choice but to allow the guard to escort him to the Bell Tower.

Cromwell showed him the appointments of the Upper Bell Tower like an indulgent host hoping to please an honoured guest, but when the door was closed and the key grated in the lock, there was no doubting the terrible reality – he was a prisoner! The only consolation was the thought that his father had once been in a similar position, and had come out of it well – and his secret? The old motto: *loyaulte me lie.* "It is my turn now," thought Wyatt, gritting his teeth, and if I am to come through this, I must adopt that motto as well. Indeed, I must remain loyal to the king, whatever I have to suffer.

NEXT DAY, CROMWELL came to visit him.

"I hope you are comfortable," he said blandly.

"Comfortable enough," said Wyatt, once again restraining a powerful urge to speak his mind. "but of course, the sooner I am free to go, the better."

Cromwell made a slight bow to show he understood.

"Very well. That is why I am here. Now, as I said yesterday, you are needed as a witness at the queen's trial."

"Her trial for...?"

"Come now, Wyatt. You know as well as I do what the charge is!"

"As a matter of fact, I don't."

"Incest, witchcraft, adultery and conspiracy against the king."

Wyatt could not help giving way to a burst of cynical laughter.

"Witchcraft! That is ridiculous!"

"Does she not have a sixth finger...?" Cromwell began, but decided for some reason to change the subject. "But there are others better qualified than you who can bear witness to that charge. What I want from you is evidence of the queen's adultery."

Wyatt froze. He knew he was on difficult ground, for had he not been Anne's lover all those years ago? He was glad, now, that he had told the king about it, but realised all too well how a man like Cromwell might use it against him. With his heart in his mouth he asked the question upon which his life might depend.

"Adultery – with whom?"

"Norris, Smeaton, Weston and Brereton."

Wyatt breathed a huge sigh of relief, though he tried not to show it. His name had not been mentioned – he might still get out of this alive!

"I want you to give evidence against them," said Cromwell.

Wyatt shook his head.

"How can I? I know nothing."

Cromwell frowned.

"Come, man! You have seen the queen in their company many times. You must have seen something."

"Nothing."

Cromwell's thin lips pursed more tightly together. It was a dangerous sign.

"Were you not there when they were laughing at the king's verses?"

Wyatt looked up in surprise. He remembered the scene, but had no idea how Cromwell had got to know of it.

"Tell, me Wyatt," said Cromwell, who saw that his words were having the desired effect, "how could any of them tell good verse from bad? You are the court poet – I suspect you were behind it."

"But..." Wyatt wanted to point out that criticising the king's verses had nothing to do with the queen's love life, but he knew very well what Cromwell was getting at. Cromwell saw his advantage and drove the point home.

"I wonder what the judges would make of that little love scene in Greenwich."

Wyatt had guessed that this would come up, but he still had now idea how to handle it. All he could do was to tell the truth.

"The King well knows what I told him before he was married."

"But if it were put before the judges..." said Cromwell, relying on this hint to do the work of many words.

Wyatt capitulated.

"Very well, Cromwell. You have me over a barrel. I will do as you say."

Did Cromwell smile at this victory? If so, his lips barely moved from the hard straight line that that was their characteristic expression.

"Then tell me what you know."

Wyatt walked over to the window to hide his exasperation.

"I've told you. I know nothing."

"Think again."

The tone in Cromwell's voice told Wyatt that he had better come up with something, or he would find himself added to the list of the accused.

"Smeaton…"

"That's better. Tell me what you know."

Wyatt went on to tell him that Mark was often in the queen's presence, seemed to sigh for her, said sweet words to her, and acted in every way like a lover. Then, with a deep breath, he told Cromwell the 'Marmalade' story. At last, with a regretful sigh, he came to the end of his narration, adding, "as for the others, I really do know nothing."

Cromwell smiled more visibly now.

"It is sufficient. It will be enough to send him to the scaffold, and as for the others, I am sure that Bryan and Page will be able to help me. Now, will you agree to repeat that evidence at the trial?"

It is a hard thing indeed to send a man to the scaffold, but Wyatt had no choice. His only comfort was the knowledge that Smeaton had already been arrested and would probably have been convicted anyway.

When Cromwell had gone, Wyatt sat down, reached for his quill and poured out his feelings in verse:

> *Was never file yet half so well yfiled,*
> *To file a file for any smith's intent,*
> *As I was made a filing instrument,*

To frame other, while that I was beguiled:
But reason, lo, hath at my folly smiled,
And pardoned me, sins that I me repent
Of my lost years, and of my time misspent.
For youth led me, and falsehood me misguided.
Yet, this trust I have of great apparence:
Since that deceit is aye returnable,
Of very force it is agreeable,
That therewithal be done the recompense:
Then guile beguiled plained should be never;
And the reward is little trust for ever.

II

On the 12th of May the trials of Norris, Smeaton, Weston and Brereton took place at Westminster Hall. Wyatt's heart sank when he saw the jury, which included men who owed Cromwell or the King a favour, and those who wanted to see the Boleyn faction brought down. The judge began the proceedings by reading out the charge:

"Henry Norris, Mark Smeaton, Francis Weston and William Brereton, you are charged with high treason. How do you plead?"

Norris, Weston and Brereton pleaded "not guilty", but Smeaton pleaded "guilty". This confirmed a rumour that Wyatt had heard that he had been put upon the rack and tortured until he confessed. If there was a confession to be held against him, there was no point in his pleading innocent. Also, it would not be Wyatt's evidence that would send him to the scaffold. This was some consolation to Wyatt, but not much. Poor Mark, his friend, his teacher, would certainly be executed, though he was sure he had done no wrong. After all, who would not confess if it was the only way to end the agony of the rack? The worse thing was that his "confession" would be used against Anne. The three other accused were gentleman, while Mark was a man of low degree. This would be seen as most shocking, for how could queen the stoop so low?

As one in a dream – or rather, nightmare – Wyatt gave his evidence, and having got it over with – for he still felt that he had perjured himself, sat back in a kind of daze to await the verdict. The jury returned a verdict of Guilty, and that the condemned men were to be divested of all lands, goods, or chattels. The judgment against all four was the same as cases of treason; execution to be at Tyburn.

In the event it was held at Tower Hill – a terrible thing for Wyatt because he could see it from a window at the Bell Tower. It was not close enough for him to witness the gory details, but he heard later how his poor friend, Mark, had stumbled on the gallows steps, then, picking himself up had said, said despairingly, "Masters, I pray you all pray for me, for I have deserved the death".

Wyatt felt sure that this suggested some arrangement with his executioners. As a man of low degree Mark was liable to be hanged, drawn and quartered, but perhaps his sentence had been commuted to the more merciful beheading on the understanding that he would make a confession at the block – thus making the case against the queen all the stronger. It seemed that Mark's resolution had failed as he climbed the steps, but thinking of that more horrible fate, he had mumbled his confession and mounted the steps to the block.

Once again, Wyatt's tortured feelings were expressed in verse. The following day he wrote a long poem in which he paid tribute to the four men who had been executed. This is what he wrote about Smeaton:

Ah! Mark, what moan should I for thee make more,
Since that thy death thou hast deserved best,

Save only that mine eye is forced sore
With piteous plaint to moan thee with the rest?
A time thou hadst above thy poor degree,
The fall whereof thy friends may well bemoan:
A rotten twig upon so high a tree
Hath slipped thy hold, and thou art dead and gone.

III

Harry, with his heart in his mouth, peeped into the kitchen. It was as he had hoped. Sally was on her own, doing the washing up. He had been trying to pluck up the courage to speak to her for months, and today he was determined to do it – or die. He had planned many fine speeches all of which began: "Sally, I love you..." but none of which seemed to come to a satisfactory conclusion. He could hardly say, "Will you marry me?" because he was too young and too poor. He thought of: "Will you be my sweetheart?" but it sounded silly. What he really wanted to say was, "Will you let me put my hand in your bodice like you did Tom Wyatt?" but he knew that wouldn't go down very well. Knowing Sally, it would probably invite a slap across the face. "Will you give me a kiss?" sounded better, but you can't just say that out of the blue, so what was he going to say? He still didn't know, but he hoped that something would come to him at the right moment. What he did know was that he was no longer going to endure sleepless nights, lying awake and sighing with lovesickness, or practicing whispering sweet nothings to Bramble while he was mucking out her stable. Mrs Goodlad, Sally's mother, would be back at any moment, so Harry knew had to seize the opportunity.

Sally was bending over a large cauldron with her back to him, attempting to clean it with a bunch of chains. It was difficult to get all the congealed fat from the bottom, and she was making slight grunting noises as she scoured. Harry came up behind her and blurted out, without preamble: "Sally, ah... er... like yer..."

She gave a sudden start and screamed with surprise. Looking round, she snapped, "Oh, it's you! What're yer thinkin' o', creepin' up on folks like that?"

Tom blushed to the roots of his hair. Sally looked magnificent in her anger with her left elbow sticking out, her hand on her hip, and in her right hand a dangerous-looking bunch of chains. Her hands were red raw, her apron wet through, and her hair bedraggled. But the wet material clung to her curves, and the untidy hair highlighted the beauty of her face. It made Tom uncomfortably aware of what a gawk of lad he was. His bony wrists stuck out from ragged shirt sleeves, and his hose were too short and full of patches.

"Ah just wanted ter tell yer that..."

"What?" she said, looking him directly in the eye.

Tom quailed, and almost lost his nerve – but he knew he had to get it over with.

"That ah... er... like yer..."

He had tried to say "love", but it came out wrong.

"Well, Harry," said Sally, in a matter-of-fact tone, "if yer like a girl yer shouldn't come creepin' up on 'er, you should 'elp 'er. An' you can 'elp me by scrubbin' aht that blasted pot!"

With that, she pushed the chains into his hand and stalked out of the kitchen. Harry looked doubtfully at the chains and wondered if his suit was prospering. Perhaps if he did a good job on the cauldron she would be nice to him, so he set to with a will.

When she came back, she looked at the cauldron and said, "Thanks, 'Arry, yer've done a grand job. Me mam'll be pleased."

The words were kind – this was his chance, and he meant to say what he felt in a way that left no room for misunderstanding.

"Well yer be me sweet'eart, Sally?"

Sally looked at him aghast. She could not have been more amazed if Harry had asked her to jump off the top of the keep.

"Sweetheart!" she scoffed. "What 'ave you got ter offer a sweetheart, Harry Maltby? Yer a gawkhammer mortal wi' no money – an' anyway, ah'm too young!"

Harry fired up at this.

"You were old enough to gu behind t' buttress wi' Tom Wyatt an' kiss 'im, an' God know what else!"

Sally's elbows went out again and her face flushed red with anger.

"It ain't true what yer say! Ah'm a good girl, ah am!"

How the argument might have developed we will never know because, just then, Mrs Goodlad popped her head round the kitchen door and said, "Ah, 'Arry, there you are!" You's wanted in t' stables."

Harry left the kitchen with a heavy heart. Everything had gone wrong from the very beginning, and, far from winning her love, he had ended up making her angry.

His master, Mr Melton, was outside the stables, waiting for him, and touch of impatience creasing his usually serene face.

"Is Bramble ready yet? I must go over to Roche Abbey to see Abbot Henry – oh, and saddle up Dobbin. I'd like you to accompany me. Hugh is needed at the gate. There's unrest brewing in Lincolnshire, and... well, better safe than sorry! If it spreads I shall have to recruit more men-at-arms – though how I will pay for them I don't know!"

Harry's ears perked up at the mention of men-at-arms. Perhaps that was the answer to his problem – if he dared ask. But of course he dared! How much easier it was to make a request of his mild-mannered master than his erstwhile sweetheart!

"Sir, would yer consider tekin' me on as a man-at-arms?"

Melton looked at Harry in surprise, but unlike his disdainful sweetheart, replied with due consideration for his feelings.

"I'm sorry, Harry, but a man-at-arms offers himself for hire complete with a horse and all his equipment – not to mention years of training."

"Ah could ride Dobbin."

Melton shook his head.

"Dobbin is a draft horse. He's big and strong, but slow – and anyway, we've no armour."

"Hugh doesn't wear much armour – only a sallet."

"But he has all the necessary equipment, and I'm sure he can be shaped up again. Believe me, he was a fine young man-at-arms when he joined the garrison fifteen years ago!"

Tom could think of nothing more to say, so he went to get the horses ready.

ROCHE ABBEY IS A RUIN today – thanks to King Henry – but even today it has a serene, other-worldly atmosphere.

Like all Cistercian foundations, it was situated well away from the nearest town, Maltby, in the Headwater Valley alongside Maltby Beck and King's Wood, and the beautiful countryside, and the lake created by damming the Beck, add to the magical quality of the place.

When they got to the abbey, Harry asked if he could have permission to visit his old tutor, Brother Boniface.

"Of course, Harry," said Melton. "I expect you will find him in the cloisters as usual."

Harry tethered the horses near the gatehouse and walked through the familiar buildings until he could hear the sound of the novices at their lessons: "*Amo, amas, amat, amamus, amatis amant*," they chanted, for knowledge of Latin was the first requirement of any educated person in those days. The novices were a mixed bunch consisting of the sons of the local nobility and wealthy burghers, along with poor boys who wanted to become monks, and waifs and strays like Harry had once been, who had no-one else to look after them. Yet, dressed as they were, in their white robes of coarse homespun, it was impossible to tell them apart, and after a few months together, the boys had almost forgotten distinctions of rank. Those who reentered the world would be reminded of them quickly enough, but the experience of living and studying together would, for the rest of their lives, give them a more humane approach to their dealings with their fellows in other ranks of society.

Brother Boniface saw Harry coming, and said to the novices, "Ah! Here is one of my former pupils – some of you may know him – no? But I am forgetting. Time flies when you get to my age. It must be five years ago at least since he last sat where you are sitting. Well then, I will give you a noun to decline and take a turn with him around the cloisters – but, look you! I shall be watching! Now, recite: *puella, puellae* – no, we don't want you thinking about girls; tables are safer, so: *mensa, mensae, mensae, mensam, mensa, mensa.*"

"That's what I could never understand," said Harry, softening his dialect in respect to his old tutor. "It's like saying: *table, table, table, table, table, table.*"

"Have you forgotten your lessons so soon? It can also mean 'meal'," Brother Boniface reminded him.

Harry laughed.

"I could never understand that, either. Can you eat a table? Can you chop vegetables on a meal?"

Brother Boniface sighed.

"You never were a scholar, Harry – but you were a wonder with animals. How do you like your job at Conisbrough Castle?"

This was the very subject Harry wanted to talk about.

"Very much, he began, except..."

"Except what?"

"I don't get paid anything. I have a place to sleep and plenty of food – but never any money."

"Then you are just like me," said Brother Boniface, "and did not Our Lord say: 'where your treasure is, there your heart will be also'?"

"But I want to get on in the world. I want to wear clothes that are better than rags. I want a place to call my own. I want a..."

"Wife," said Brother Boniface interrupting him to get to the point.

Harry looked at him aghast. Had somebody been telling tales? No, how could they? The only other person who knew his secret was Sally.

"So that's where your heart is – Sally, is it not?"

How could Brother Boniface know so much? Was it true that he practised the Black Arts in a hidden crypt below the nave? – That's what his fellow novices used to say when they were caught out for some misdemeanour. But Harry knew better, now. Somehow, the very unworldliness of the monks gave them a surprising depth of insight into worldly affairs. Brother Boniface had simply applied his Aristotelian logic to the situation. After all, why else would a young man want to better himself, and what other young girls did Harry see on a day to day basis? So it was better to confess, and hope that help would be forthcoming.

"Yes."

Brother Boniface considered the situation while they took another turn round the cloisters. As they passed the boys, he gave the plural of *mensa* to recite, and then returned to his thoughts. By the time they got to the opposite end of the cloister, he had worked out his answer.

"Harry, I don't suppose it is worth trying to persuade you once again to give up the world and join the abbey. Of course, you can never be a monk because, to be honest, I don't think you will ever learn Latin – let alone the complexities of Theology, but you can be a Lay Brother. We could do with somebody like you in charge of our stables."

Harry shook his head.

"Very well. It is possible to serve The Lord in the world as well as in the cloister, so I will do what I can to help you. I will ask around in Maltby and Tickhill to see if I can find an apprenticeship to a Farrier or Blacksmith, and I will ask your master if he will do the same in Conisbrough. A master Farrier or Blacksmith will be a good catch for a humble kitchen maid – so I'm sure you will get your Sally, after all."

Harry was pleased with this, though he wished he could feel as sure about Sally as Brother Boniface.

ON THE WAY BACK, MELTON seemed melancholy. He had not intended to discuss his concerns with Harry, his servant, but it came out anyway.

"Abbot Henry is worried about the future of the Abbey and so am I, Harry."

"What do you mean?" replied Harry.

"For two years, now, the king and his first minister have been seeking for ways to redirect ecclesiastical income to the benefit of the Crown."

That meant little to Harry. Everybody he knew was short of money. He had none, Hugh had had little, and Melton did not have enough to staff the castle, or repair dilapidations – so it was not surprising that the king was short of money too.

"But we fear it will not stop until the king seizes everything – but I have said too much already."

Harry was troubled by this news.

"But why would t' king do that? The monasteries do a lot o' good. They feed t' poor, heal t' sick, pray for our souls, an'... well, if it weren't fer Roche Abbey ah'd probably not be 'ere!" said Harry, forgetting his manners and lapsing back into the broad dialect.

Melton shook his head.

"But we hope and pray that it won't come to that."

"Aye," agreed Harry. "Hope and pray."

That news made his own problems seem petty, and for the first time in many months, he lay awake thinking of something other than Sally.

IV

One of the worst days for Wyatt was the day of Anne's trial because, though there could be no outcome but one, he was tormented by hope – something, perhaps, would happen to save her, some brave, unbiased witness, or a change of heart on King Henry's part – something, anything – but not the condemnation of his Anne, his lover, stolen by the king, who now sought to be rid of her.

He paced up and down his cell all day, waiting for news. Sometimes he would sit down, take his quill and try to find relief in poetry – but nothing came except fragments:

> *The high mountains are blasted oft*
> *When the low valley is mild and soft...*
>
> *The fall is grievous from aloft,*
> *And sure, circa Regna tonat....*
>
> *These bloody days have broken my heart,*
> *My lust, my youth did them depart...*

For a man of action, like Wyatt, it was very hell to be trapped there, unable to do anything to help his former lover – but it is just as well that he was, for his emotions had been screwed to such a pitch that he would, without doubt, have lost his head and.... lost his head.

At last his gaoler arrived with a platter of food, and what was infinitely more important – news. To Wyatt's urgent request he replied in a solemn tone: "The jury convicted."

"Oh what grounds?" said Wyatt through gritted teeth – though he knew well enough, for had not he helped to supply them?

"Adultery, treason... Mind you, she spoke well in her own defence, and admitted nothing. Her brother, Brereton, spoke well too, so well that it looked as though he might be acquitted."

"And was he?"

"No."

Wyatt breathed a heavy sigh, and the gaoler beat a hasty retreat in case he should be asked any more awkward questions. He knew well enough that the only way to survive in King Henry's court was to see little and say less.

As soon as he had locked the door, Wyatt, in an outburst of pent-up frustration, kicked over the table, sending his dinner clattering to the floor.

But worse was to come – much worse! Anne's execution took place soon after, and was held inside the Tower grounds, meaning that poor Wyatt had a grandstand view of his former lover's execution. He saw her led from her prison to the scaffold, ashen faced, resigned, but courageous. She climbed up to the block, said a few words, resolutely asserting her innocence, and then made her preparations. She said a prayer, tied her hair back, fastened her dress around her feet (so that her legs would not splay open in the throes of death) and gave gold to the executioner. Then, with quiet dignity, she laid her head on the block – did Wyatt remember how that fair head had once lain beside him on a pillow at Greenwich? – Perhaps so, but his thoughts and feelings were too confused to make space for any clear recollections. All he knew was that he wanted to reverse time and to go back the days when he had first met her. Then he would whisk her away from court and take her to some remote place where the king would never see her. But it was too late! – too late! The axe fell, wielded by an expert swordsman brought especially from Calais, so they said, as a mark of the king's clemency. The blow was clean, the head fell, the blood gushed, and a great roar arose from the crowd. Wyatt staggered away from the window, threw himself on his bed, and sobbed his heart out.

Later, when his seething emotions had settled a little, he put together some of his poetic fragments and wrote a poem. The first version (and the second and third) were so outspoken that he threw them on the fire. Finally, he managed to produce a powerful, yet subtle expression of feelings that expressed his criticisms in general terms, the 'circa Regna tonat', 'storms hover around kings' being an expression that could apply to any king, not just Henry VIII.

> *The high mountains are blasted oft*
> *When the low valley is mild and soft,*
> *Fortune with Health stands at debate,*
> *The fall is grievous from aloft,*
> *And sure, circa Regna tonat.*
>
> *These bloody days have broken my heart,*

My lust, my youth did them depart,
And blind desire of estate.
Who hastes to climb seeks to revert,
Of truth, circa Regna tonat.

The bell tower showed me such a sight
That in my head sticks day and night.
There did I learn out of a grate,
For all favour, glory, might,
That yet, circa Regna tonat.

V

The Pilgrimage of Grace was gathering momentum. It had begun in Lincolnshire, led by Moreland and Borrowby, and spread rapidly throughout the northern counties under a new leader called Thomas Aske. Its purpose was to make a peaceful protest in favour of Catholicism and against the dissolution of the monasteries.

The more Harry heard about it, the more he felt that he would like to join the Pilgrimage and try to save what he held most dear – after Sally, of course! But he found himself thinking less and less about Sally, and more and more about the Pilgrimage. His dreams were haunted now, not by Sally's golden curls, full lips, and inviting bodice, but by Brother Boniface's tonsure, pursed lips and coarse woollen habit – was the king really planning to dissolve him? The only kind of 'dissolve' that Harry knew about was when sugar dissolves in water, and he imagined poor Brother Boniface being dissolved in the same way, along with Abbot Henry and all the monks at Roche Abbey.

It troubled him so much that he decided that he must seek Brother Boniface's advice. The only way to do this was to get up well before dawn and try to get back to Conisbrough before he was missed. He still remembered the times of the daily offices, and knew that he would be able to catch Brother Boniface emerging from the Abbey Church after matins, which ended at dawn.

So, in the black of the early hours, Harry slipped out of his pallet in the attic above the kitchen, and crept to the main gate. There was nobody on guard, Hugh only being able to perform that duty in daylight hours. Harry slid back the rusty bolts as quietly as he could (which was not very quietly) and hurried to the Barbican gate, where he did the same. The gatehouse of the outer bailey was a crumbled ruin, so there was nothing to do there.

A sliver of a moon gave enough light to see the roads, and soon Harry was on his way to Tickhill. He had considered taking Dobbin, but that would have caused too much disturbance. In any case, it was only about five miles – no distance at all to his strong, young legs. A few years ago he would have been too afraid to have undertaken such a long walk at night. The thought of ghosts and goblins, robbers and Robin Hood would have kept him safe in the castle, but now he was old enough to have abandoned his childish belief in ghosts and goblins, and wise enough to know that no robber would waste his time on Conisbrough folk, who had nothing worth stealing. As for Robin Hood, he knew from the old ballads that he was only interested in rich knights and overfed abbots.

BROTHER BONIFACE WAS surprised to see him at such an early hour, but gave him good greeting nevertheless.

"I need your advice," said Harry, coming to the point quickly, as he knew he must get back to the castle as soon as possible.

Brother Boniface replied with a deprecating laugh.

"Harry, surely you know that I am the last person – with my vow of chastity – to help you in your suit?"

"No, it's not about Sally," said Harry. "I want your advice about the Pilgrimage."

"Well?" said Brother Boniface, raising his bushy eyebrows with surprise.

"I want to join," said Harry simply.

Brother Boniface did not need a turn about the cloisters to come to a conclusion about this problem.

"Then join."

"But if I do, I'll be betraying Mr Melton."

"How so?"

"Because the castle is the king's and is against the pilgrimage."

Brother Boniface frowned. He saw the difficulty, though it still didn't need a turn about the cloisters.

"Remember the words of Our Lord: 'Render unto Caesar that which is Caesar's, and unto God that which is God's. Sometimes our duty to God overrides our duty to Caesar – but that is for you to decide."

"I had already decided, but I wanted to know what you thought about it."

Brother Boniface's usually serene expression crumpled with concern.

"I fear that our king is a victim of evil counsel – and I will go so far as to name the villain – one Thomas Cromwell. He has connived at the downfall of the True Church for the worst of reasons – not because, like the Lutherians, he holds a different belief, but to fill the king's coffers, and in so doing, to advance himself – ah! Would that our order had kept to our founder's intention and remained poor!"

"But you are poor," said Harry, "every one of you."

"The monks are poor, yes, but the abbey is rich. It happened almost by accident. Our founder sought a place remote from human habitation so that we could live simply, well away from the temptations of the world. Our predecessors worked hard. The lands they farmed became rich, so they built this magnificent church to the glory of God – and now the covetous eyes of worldly men have found us out!"

"Will you join the Pilgrimage, Brother Boniface?"

Brother Boniface shook his head firmly.

"No. We have a better way to fight the Philistines..."

Harry looked at him with eager, hopeful eyes.

"...prayer..."

Harry was disappointed, though he knew he shouldn't be.

"...we are praying day and night that the evil counsellor will receive his just deserts and that the king will show mercy to his servants."

Brother Boniface looked at Harry with a question in his eyes. It was a question he had asked so often that he didn't need to put it into words. Nor did Harry need to answer. He simply shook his head and said, "Then I will join the Pilgrimage. Will you give me your blessing, Brother?"

Brother Boniface placed his hand on Harry's head and spoke some words in Latin, then added, "and I'll also give you some advice. Father Ermystead of St Peter's is also minded to join the Pilgrimage. Go to see him. He may, perhaps, allow you to join his band, and then at least you will be safe from the perils of the highway – getting lost being the most likely."

He was right, for apart from a very few old Roman milestones, there were no signs of any kind. Most people in those days did not travel, and those who did knew where they were going.

Tom felt much better after those few words from Brother Boniface, and as he hurried back to Conisbrough, began to make his plans.

It was still early when he got to the main gatehouse, but not early enough to beat Hugh, who usually started his day there as it was the nearest guard post to the guard house.

"An' where 'ave you been at this time in t' mornin'?" he said, suspiciously.

"Dahn ter t' mill," said Harry, saying the first thing that came into his head, and seeing that Hugh was not convinced, added, "T' maister sent me."

"Aye, well, tha'd best get rahnd ter t' stables an' get them 'osses mucked aht."

That job could wait, thought Harry. In the meantime, he had something more important to see to. He hurried to the kitchen and hovered around until Mrs Goodlad went out to attend to some other duty, then made a beeline for Sally.

Sally looked up from her pastry making, sighed and said, "Nah then, 'Arry, ah'm busy. Ah've got no time for sweetheart talk."

"It was not that that ah wanted to see yer abaht," said Harry quickly.

Was that a look of disappointment that flitted over Sally's fair features? Yes, but not disappointed love, for she didn't think much of Harry as a lover, it was more a case of disappointed vanity – for every woman likes to have a suitor, regardless of what she thinks of him.

"Well then?"

"Ah'm thinkin' o' joinin' t' Pilgrimage."

Sally was aghast. She turned round to face him with the rolling pin still in one hand as though she meant to hit him over the head with it.

"Tha's daft!" she exclaimed.

"No, ah'm not," said Harry. "It's t' least ah can do ter repay what t' monks 'ave done for me. You know my story, 'ow ah were abandoned outside Roche Abbey gatehouse when a were nobbut a babby, 'ow they took me in and eddicated me, an' foun' me this place."

"Aye," said Sally, a note of understanding in her voice. "But if yer gu on t' Pilgrimage, yer'll likely lose yer place – an' then what'll yer do, 'Arry Maltby?"

"Ah'm not worried abaht that. Father Boniface said he'll apprentice me to a Farrier in Tickhill – but ah'll be sorry to let Mr Melton down, for he's bin a good maister."

Sally looked at Harry with surprise. She was seeing a new side of him. Was this the same gawky, clumsy, awkward lad who had made such a botched attempt at love making only a few days ago? His gawky appearance had not changed, but now he seemed stronger, wiser and more confident – and what was that about being an apprentice? Perhaps Harry would make something of himself, after all, and perhaps his lovemaking was not something to be laughed at.

"Why're yer tellin' me all this?"

"Cos someb'dy in t' castle should know where ah've gone. Listen. Ah'm goin' ter tek off one mornin' early, an' nob'dy will miss us fer a while. What ah want you ter do is cover fer me as long as yer can – yer know what ah mean – someb'dy asks, 'Weer's 'Arry?' and you reply, 'Ah saw 'im a minute ago', or summat like that. Then, when yer can't cover it it no longer, tell 'em ah've gone ter join t' Pilgrimage at York."

"What! You expect me ter tell a load of fibs just to cover your sneaky back?" expostulated Sally.

"Come on, Sal. It's for the True Church, for the monasteries – for Brother Boniface."

If Harry had asked for a kiss he could not have been making a greater demand, but at least she could have coped with that – by sending him packing with a few sharp words.

"Ah don't know."

Harry sighed. He had counted on Sally's help. Hugh would report him, Mrs Goodlad would tell Hugh, and as for Mr Melton – yes, that was it, if Sally wouldn't help he would have to make a clean breast of it to Mr Melton. He was a kind, understanding man, and had not been able to hide his sympathy with the Pilgrimage.

"All reet, Sally," said Harry, "Ah'll not press yer. Ah'll 'ave to see Mr Melton, that's all. Ah canna just tek off an' leave 'im worryin' abaht me."

Once again, Sally felt that Harry had turned the tables on her. He had asked her for something more important than a kiss, and when she had hesitated, he had thought of an alternative. On an impulse she said, "Ah'll help yer, 'Arry. Tell me again what ah've ter do."

PART 3

"Such hap as I am happed in..."

I

I t had been a chilly day, and Hugh, still the only man-at-arms in Conisbrough Castle, was sheltering under the arch of the gatehouse, well back from the gate, which stood open. He was sitting on his three-legged stool and lounging against the wall, when he heard the clatter of hooves in the Barbican. Quickly, he jumped to attention, put on his sallet, and picked up the halberd which was leaning against the wall nearby. Then, just in time, he rang the bell to alert his master, and took up a soldierly stance at the gate.

To his bewilderment, he saw a long train of armed men marching two by two, followed by a lumbering supply waggon. At their head were two armed men on horseback with shields bearing a strange coat of arms with six panels bearing a cross, a lion rampant, a chevron, a boar's head, and a device he had never seen before and couldn't identify. However, there was something familiar about the two men at the head of the column, and as they came up the steep slope towards the main gate, he recognised them as Thomas Wyatt and his son. Nevertheless, he barred the way and gave the challenge: "In the name of king, state your name and business."

"Thomas Wyatt on the king's business."

"Then pass."

Hugh stood aside and watched with fascinated disbelief as twenty men-at-arms, all better equipped than him – real men-at-arms in fact – marched past him.

Harry had arrived to help with the horses, and Melton, the seneschal, was not far behind him.

"I thought you were imprisoned in the Tower," said Melton to Wyatt.

"I was, but thanks to Cromwell and my father I'm a free man. What's more, the king has entrusted me with two new posts."

"Which are?"

"Constable of Kent – and Constable of this castle, jointly with my son."

"Congratulations to you both. I am glad of it. That makes three generations of Wyatts as the constable of this castle. It could be in no better hands."

Wyatt gave a slight nod of his head in acknowledgment. It was then that Melton noticed the coat of arms.

"I see that was not all the king gave you," he said with a gesture towards Wyatt's shield.

Wyatt smiled. "Indeed, I came out of the whole sorry business rather well, and was knighted for my loyalty. See..."

He pointed at the strange device that Hugh had not recognised. "Here is the horse barnacle, the symbol of Wyatt loyalty. The other devices represent various branches of my family."

"But, why the men-at-arms?"

"I am commanded by the king to garrison this castle against the northern rebels."

"You mean, The Pilgrimage of Grace," said Melton, like a teacher correcting a pupil.

"Ah!" said Wyatt, musingly, "the power of words. They are the same people, but 'rebels' are one thing, and 'pilgrims' are quite another."

"'Pilgrims' is the right word, for their protest is peaceful."

"The king sees them as rebels, and I am loyal to the king."

There was a steely, determined look in Wyatt's eyes as he said this, as though the poet had been pushed away by the man of action.

A commotion at the barbican gatehouse distracted Melton for a moment, and seeing what was happening, he said to Hugh, "Tell them that they'll never get that waggon up here. They should leave it in the Outer Bailey – but be sure to unload it before it gets dark."

With some trepidation, Hugh, the least man-at-armly of the all the men-at-arms in England, marched down to the barbican gatehouse and started giving orders.

"Tha can't get that up 'ere. Nah, put it 'ard by an' gerrit unloaded, or t' townsfolk'll unload it for thee. An' get them 'osses up to t' stables. They look done in!"

Melton turned his attention back to Wyatt, and said, "But why did you bring those the men-at-arms?"

"It seems that the rebellion is spreading to Yorkshire, by all accounts. York and Hull have opened their gates to Aske, so I have orders to repair and garrison this castle, and hold it against the rebels."

"With 20 men?"

"These men-at-arms are the advance guard, more will follow. Tickhill is being garrisoned in the same way – 200 men, with ordinance, under the command of my old friend Bryan."

"How many are coming here?"

"I have 150 Kentmen on the king's commission."

"150! But where will we put them all?"

"In the outer bailey."

"But there is no outer bailey – you know that!"

"That's what these men-at-arms are for – oh, not to do the work, of course. They are here to organise working parties. We'll start with the Castlegardurn men. They will be told that they must offer service either in person or by proxy, but that the Castlegardurn tax will no longer be accepted in lieu. We will garrison my men in the buildings along the south curtain..."

"But you know full well that they are in a dangerous state!"

"Well, I dare say that they'll stay up a bit longer. Tom, bring Serjeant Bosville, and Hugh, if you can find him."

Moments later the two men-at-arms were standing side by side in front of him – and a greater contrast could not be imagined. Hugh's sallet was dull and pitted. His hair and beard were unkempt, his jupon was frayed and faded, and his pot belly bulged over his sword belt. Serjeant Bosville, on the other hand, was the epitome of serjeant-at-armliness. He was strong and fit, his beard was neatly trimmed, his helmet and armour had been polished till they gleamed, and his jupon was freshly laundered.

"Hugh, I am promoting you to serjeant-at-arms of Conisbrough Castle," said Wyatt. "You know the castle well, and it is up to you to organise the guard duties, and the Castlegardurn men when they arrive. Serjeant Bosville, of course, will retain overall command. Melton, can you find Hugh a better outfit?"

"Leave that to me, sire," said Serjeant Bosville. "We have arms and armour in the waggon."

"Very well, and now that is settled, Melton, what about some of your famous Conisbrough hospitality?"

Melton looked all at sixes and sevens, and Wyatt guessed why. He took a handful of gold from his purse and gave it to Melton.

"On the king's commission. Now, I could eat a horse! Set Mrs Goodlad and Sally about it."

But they needed no telling. Sally and her mother had watched the arrivals from the kitchen window.

"There's yer man-at-arms, duck," said Mrs Goodlad.

"What do yer mean?" said Sally, who, to her mother's surprise, seemed to be thinking of something else.

"I thought you was after a man-at-arms to marry?"

"I am."

"Well, then, look!"

Sally looked, and though she had never seen so many young, strong men together, she didn't seem to be impressed – perhaps she had thoughts of somebody else lurking in her heart.

"What about 'im?" said Mrs Goodlad, referring to a young man-at-arms who had just glanced at their window.

"'Ee's all reet, mam."

"All reet! 'Ee's got more about 'im than any 'o t' lads in town, an' ah bet 'ee's on two shillin' a day – not like yer dad, who's only a garrison guard. Ah'd 'ave 'im – but then, ah'd 'ave 'em all! Only jestin' mind yer! Don't tell yer dad!"

They both had a good, long laugh at this until suddenly Mrs Goodlad said, "Upon me word! 'Ere's us yakkin' like a couple o' Whitby fishwives an' that lot'll want feedin'. Nah then, ah'll rustle summat up for the gen'lemen, while you 'urry into town ter see if yer can get us a couple o' fat porkers for t' men-at-arms. No, wait a mo'. Yer gettin' to be a big girl, an' you know what them Conisbrough lads is like. I'll gu mesen, an' I'll ask maister for the wherewithal afore I gu."

Just then, her husband popped his head round the kitchen door.

"'Ave yer seen 'Arry? He's wanted at t' stables?"

"Nay, ah a'n't seen 'im all mornin'. 'Ave you, lass?"

"I'n't he in t' stables?" said Sally, guessing that this was the moment that Harry had prepared her for.

"Mebbe," said Hugh, unconcernedly. "Ah'll 'ave a look."

Just then, young Tom appeared behind Hugh and asked him something about the guardroom. He caught Sally's eye and winked at her. She blushed, shuffled uncomfortably, and looked away.

"Well, never mind about 'Arry," continued Hugh, "Ah've to go to t' guardroom with t' young maister. But if tha sees 'im, tha'd best send 'im straight to me."

With that, he was gone, leaving his daughter to stare wistfully at the young man who had interrupted them.

"Ah, so that's the way the land lies, is it, yer brazen hussy?" said Mrs Goodlad, who had missed nothing. "Yer'll get noweer wi' 'im, mark my words! If yer've got any sense, yer'll set yer cap at one them men-at-arms like ah did when ah was your age – but we a'n't got time for that nah, we've got an army ter feed!"

II

That evening, the great hall in Conisbrough Castle bailey was livelier than it had been for many a long year. At the high table sat Wyatt and his son, along with the seneschal, Melton. Below them sat the twenty men-at-arms, and near the door and the draught, the fletcher, the farrier and the armourer.

Mrs Goodlad and Sally toiled away in the kitchen to supply the seemingly endless string of requests from the tables, and the pages and squires who brought them.

"Well, ah'm fagged to to death!" said Mrs Goodlad, brushing the sweat from her brow with her apron.

One of the pages, who had come to collect a platter of roasted nightingales, laughed and said, "Just you wait till the others get here."

"What others?" she said.

"Haven't you heard – there's another 150 men-at-arms expected soon, not to mention the squires, pages, archers, fletchers, farriers, blacksmiths and assorted varlets."

"What!" gasped Mrs Goodlad. "Why that's more folk than in the whole of Conisbrough!"

"Well, you've got to cook for 'em!"

Mrs Goodlad was so overwhelmed at the thought that she collapsed onto a little three-legged stool near the kitchen table, only to be hurried onto her feet again by another page who rushed in calling for venison.

At the high table the conversation was grave.

"It's good to see the old castle come to life again," said Melton, "but I hope it will not come to a siege."

"The place is invincible," said Wyatt. "That keep must be the strongest in England. I've never seen walls so thick! I can't imagine what enemy they were planning to keep out! "

"Nevertheless," said Melton, "Conisbrough is not invincible. It has been under siege before – and was taken."

"I find that hard to believe. When was that?"

"A long time ago, in 1317, I think. Thomas Lancaster laid siege to the castle, and took it by undermining the south curtain."

"Which would explain the state it is in today."

"Yes, it was never properly repaired."

Wyatt was thoughtful. "I will take a close look at it tomorrow and see what can be done."

Melton fell silent after that, as though something was on his mind that he was reluctant to talk about.

"Modern artillery would have the walls down in no time," said Tom.

Wyatt shook his head. "Perhaps the curtain walls, but those bastions, and the keep, are so thick, they could hammer away at them all day and make no difference. No, Tom. Don't be so quick to dismiss the strength of a castle. In any case, I've heard that the rebels have no artillery."

"They've got plenty of men, though," said young Tom. "30,000 at the last count!"

"And the right." Melton mumbled the words, half apologetically, spluttering on his food as he did so. It was as though the words came out without him wanting them to.

Wyatt looked hard at him. "What do you mean?"

Melton swallowed his mouthful, and took a deep draft of wine, which seemed to bolster his courage. "The dissolving of the monasteries is wrong. Look at the good they do! They heal the sick, they feed the starving, they shelter travellers, and above all, they pray for our souls. Look at Roche Abbey. The abbot, Henry, is as holy a man as you could wish to meet. That abbey has succoured the folk of South Yorkshire for generations. Young Harry is a good example. He was abandoned as a baby and the monks took him in."

"It is only the smaller houses that are being dissolved," said Wyatt. "The good work of the larger houses will continue."

"But we all fear that they will be next."

"Well, I agree with King Henry," said Tom. "We English have had enough of the Pope lording it over us."

But his father said nothing. He stared at the food on his plate, though his thoughts were far away as he struggled with conflicting feelings. At last he said, interrupting his son's diatribe against the Pope, "I am not without sympathy for the rebels, but I am guided by one principle in life. You know what it is, Melton. We have talked of it before."

"Yes," said Melton. "Your motto: *loyaulte me lie.*"

"Yes. And I am loyal to the king."

"Despite what I heard..."

"Don't speak of it... Yes, despite everything. And as my constable, that is what I expect from you. We must put this castle in a defensive state, and we must prepare to accommodate a garrison of 150 men-at-arms, plus squires, pages, archers, fletchers, farriers, blacksmiths and assorted varlets. I hope – pray – that it will not come to a fight, but if it does, we must be prepared to lay down our lives for the king."

Melton shook his head sadly, but after a moment, replied, "Well, Wyatt, I have my own bond of loyalty and it is to this castle. This castle is the king's, and so I am the king's man. You can count on me – yes, even unto death. Though my heart and my soul is with Pilgrimage of Grace."

"That's enough for me," said Wyatt. "Now, let us turn to more pleasant matters.

Tom had already turned his mind to more pleasant matters, for the shortage of pages meant that Sally had been sent to refill the decanters on the high table. She had taken off her stained kitchen apron, brushed her hair, and shuffled down the front of her gown to reveal a glimpse of the ripe fruit inside. As she leaned forward to refill young Tom's glass, he looked at the view appreciatively and whispered a few private words to her. Melton noticed this, and said, "Sally, what are you doing here? You should be in the kitchen helping your mother."

Sally made a demure courtesy and replied sweetly, "But there aren't enough pages, sir."

"Where is Harry?"

Sally looked uncomfortable and said nothing.

"Well?"

"He must be very busy with all those extra horses, I think, sir."

"Sir Thomas brought his own farrier."

"Well, I'm, sure he's around somewhere," said Sally, who feared that the moment of truth was nigh.

"Send Hugh to me, perhaps he knows."

Sally courtesied again and left the table. She was back again in no time carrying a blackbird pie which, though it contained fewer than the four-and-twenty blackbirds of the children's song, looked delicious enough, and perhaps gave Wyatt the idea of asking if there was a chance of any musical entertainment.

"A good idea!" said Melton. "That's what we used to do in the old days. Is there a minstrel among your men?"

The question was passed around, but after much shaking of heads, the answer came back – no.

"You're quite the musician, Sir Thomas. Why don't you give us a tune?"

Wyatt shook his head. "Perhaps it is better if I keep my dignity as a peer of the realm. My son, here can play for us. Go and get the lute, Tom."

"Glad to, father, though I've not been learning long, and you know I'm no singer. A cat's chorus sounds sweeter."

"I can sing," chimed in a sweet little voice from the side of the table.

They all looked. It was Sally. Melton immediately said, "What, are you still here? Begone girl! Your mother can't cope all by herself."

"Wait," said Wyatt. "If she can sing. Let her stay. What can you sing, girl?"

"Oh, only the old folk songs."

"That'll do. It's not Hampton Court, after all."

Just then young Tom returned with the lute, adjusted the tuning, and said, "What shall it be, Sally?"

"What about *Outlandish Knight*, sir?"

"I don't know that one."
"Well, what about *Bushes and Briars?*"
Young Tom struck a chord and Sally began to sing.

> *Through bushes and briars*
> *I've lately made my way*
> *All for to hear the small birds sing*
> *And the lambs to skip and play*
>
> *I overheard a my own true love*
> *Her voice it rang so clear*
> *Long time have I been waiting for*
> *The coming of my dear*
>
> *Sometimes I am uneasy*
> *And troubled in my mind*
> *Sometimes I think I'll go to him*
> *And tell to him my mind.*
>
> *But if I should go to my love*
> *My love he would say nay*
> *If I showed to him my boldness*
> *He'd ne'er love me again*

Her voice was sweeter than the blackbirds that they had eaten with such relish, and was made even more poignant by the way she stole an occasional glance at young Tom. The words, perhaps, were a reflection of her feelings, and the audience seemed to sense it. Wyatt was particularly affected by the song, so affected, that tears sprang to his eyes. He was remembering what he had been trying so hard to forget:

The bell tower showed me such a sight
That in my head sticks day and night.

When the song ended, there was a moment of absolute silence followed by tumultuous applause and calls for another song, and another, until the fire was flickering low in the great hooded fireplace.

Hugh was standing in the shadows waiting for the best moment to approach the high table. He had not wanted to interrupt his master during the singing, but as soon as it was over, he went up to the high table and said to the seneschal in a low voice.

"Harry is missing, sire. Nobody has seen him all day, and I can't find him anywhere."

Sally overheard. She looked quickly at her father, and then hurried away. Hugh knew his daughter all too well, and guessed that she knew something about it. He hurried after and caught up with her in the kitchen, where he grabbed her wrist, and said in his gruff man-at-armly voice: "Nah then, madam. Tell me what yer know."

"Ah dunna know owt," she said, reverting to the broad dialect in her defiance.

Hugh squeezed her wrist harder.

"Ow! Yer 'urtin' me!"

He squeezed harder still.

"Tell!"

"'Ee's gone ter join t' Pilgrimage."

"What? When?"

"This mornin'. 'Ee wanted someb'dy ter know weer 'ee were guin' but 'ee told me ter keep it secret as long as possible."

"Which way did 'ee go?"

"York."

Hugh let go of his daughter's wrist and slapped her face. Not hard, but hard enough to leave a big red mark and bring tears to her eyes."

"Aye! An tha'll get another one from me if tha dusna' stop mooning arahnd t' young maister!" said her mother who had been listening with an angry scowl on her face.

The noise woke Totty up and she started crying.

"Nah look what tha's done! Waken' t' babby! Ah dun't know 'ow ah can cope, wi' me 'avin' to to cook for all them folk an' no'b'dy ter 'elp wi' Totty! Yer'd best stay 'ere, nah, an' try an' settle 'er dahn."

Hugh hurried back to the hall to report to Melton and to ask permission to go after him. Melton shook his head.

"It's no good, Hugh. If he went this morning, he'll be well on his way. He might even be there. You'll never find him, and you're needed here."

Hugh was about to protest, but Melton continued: "God willing he will come to no harm, and will come back to his in his own good time."

"Aye, an' when 'ee does... well, ah shall be pleased to see 'im, but by 'r Lady, ah'll teach him a lesson, ah will. Ah'll throw 'im in t' dungeon!"

Harry's disappearance cast a gloom over the high table. The lute was put away, and Wyatt announced that he was ready for bed. He made his way up the stairs, followed by his son, saw him settled down, and then sought the privacy of his own chamber. No sooner had he sat on his bed than nightmare scenes from the Tower flooded his mind. The most moving was the scene of his lover, Anne, kneeling to the block. He sank his head in his hands and wept like a child.

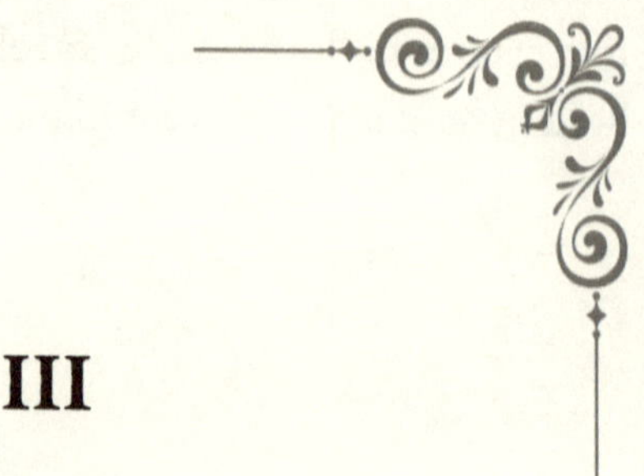

III

Harry had been wrestling with his conscience for weeks, but when the advance guard turned up he knew that it was now or never. The new arrivals created a confusion that would allow him time to get well away before anybody realised he was gone. Also, he had heard that a band of Pilgrims from Conisbrough was to set out that very morning from St Peter's Church.

He would be sorry to let the seneschal down, as he had been a good master, and even sorrier to desert Hugh and his wife, who had been like his mother and father, but he could never forget that he owed his life to the monks of Roche Abbey, who had looked after him when he had been abandoned. As he had grown up in their care, he had experienced at first hand all the good that the monks did. They fed the hungry, cared for the sick, and offered education to boys for the priesthood or other professions.

He had planned his escape carefully, but even though he had recruited Sally as a helper, he had not told her the whole truth. He told her that he would head for York, though he was planning to go in the opposite direction, to Pontefract, where he had heard that the pilgrims were gathering.

He sneaked out of the castle under cover of the new arrivals and headed straight for St Peter's Church. There he found Father Ermystead saying prayers with a group of pilgrims, many of whom he recognised. As soon as they realised he was a fellow pilgrim, they welcomed him with open arms.

"Come along with us, lad," said Father Ermystead. "There's safety in numbers. It's 15 mile if it's an inch, but if we step out boldly we'll be there by nightfall."

Along the way Harry fell into conversation with some of his fellow pilgrims.

"It's a terrible thing the king's duin'," said one, a farm lad who went by the name of Barley-O.

"Aye," said another. "'Ee's ordered that the churches should be pulled down!"

"And men taxed for christening and marriage," said a third.

Harry shouted a protest. "That's not fair! It's worse than ah thought!"

But Father Ermystead heard the commotion and went to find out what it was all about. Tom told him, but the vicar shook his head. "You don't need to worry about those things. They're just foolish rumours. The truth is bad enough."

"Begging your pardon," said Harry, "but what *is* the truth? Ah 'eard that the king was going to close the monasteries."

"You heard right," said Father Ermystead, "and that is the worse of it, but there's the Ten Articles and the new order of prayer issued by Thomas Cranmer."

Harry shook his head. "Ah know nothin' o' that."

"Well, put simply, they are part of the process of breaking away from the Church of Rome."

"Is it true that the king wants ter take away all t' church plate an' melt it dahn into gold bars fer his coffers?" asked Barley-O.

Father Ermystead shook his head. "No, no. That's just another false rumour. Though the king will certainly confiscate the assets of the religious houses that he closes."

"So 'ee *will* take our plate! – well, some of it. Lads, the king is going ter take away our church plate!"

"No, no!" protested Father Ermystead. But the new rumour was already spreading.

Pontefract Castle was a revelation to Harry, it being three times the size of Conisbrough Castle, with an imposing array of high towers, topped by numerous tourelles, from which armed guards scanned the landscape.

More like a castle found in France
Or chronicle of old romance

is how the old poem describes it – not that they could get anywhere near the castle itself. It was surrounded by a city of tents which accommodated the attendants of the hundreds of peers, knights and gentry who had flocked to Pontefract in support of the pilgrimage.

"It looks as though t' trees'll be our roof toneet," said Barley-O.

"Yes, so pray the rain keeps off," said Father Ermystead.

While they were finding places to settle down, Father Ermystead met with the leaders of other groups of pilgrims to discuss what they should do next. When he returned, he asked the Conisbrough men to join a large crowd of other pilgrims in an open field nearby. When they arrived at the field they were all asked to kneel and to take the pilgrim's oath. It was recited a line at a time by Edward Lee, the Archbishop of York, magnificent in his full regalia:

> *Ye shall not enter into this our Pilgrimage of Grace for the common wealth but only for the love ye bear to God's faith and church militant and the maintenance thereof, the preservation of the king's person, his issue, and the purifying of the nobility and to expulse all villein blood and evil counsellors against the common wealth of the same. And that ye shall not enter into our said pilgrimage for no peculiar private profit to no private person but by counsel of the common wealth nor slay nor murder for no envy but in your hearts to put away all fear for the common wealth. And to take before you the cross of Christ and your heart's faith to the restitution of the church and to the suppression of heretics' opinions by the holy content of this book.*

Taking the oath left Harry with a feeling that he had somehow been lifted up above earthly things, and that everything was now blessed and holy.

It was late October, and evening came early, along with a bitter wind. The Conisbrough pilgrims, like the others, made a fire and huddled round for warmth. One pilgrim produced a loaf of bread, another some strips of dried beef, and another some fresh eggs. Those who had nothing offered to go to the River Aire to bring water, and so, like the Miracle of the

Feeding of the 5,000, the mutual good will ensured that no-one went hungry to his bed under the stars.

As Harry wrapped himself in his cloak and settled down to sleep he could hear the voices of other pilgrims in other groups not far way singing the pilgrim's hymn:

> *Christ crucified!*
> *For thy wounds wide,*
> *Us commons guide!*
> *Which pilgrims be,*
> *Through God's grace,*
> *For to purchase*
> *Old wealth and peace*
> *Of the spirituality.*
>
> *Great God's fame*
> *Doth Church proclaim*
> *Now to be lame*
> *And fast in bonds,*
> *Robbed, spoiled, and shorn*
> *From cattle and corn,*
> *And clean forth borne*
> *Of house and lands.*
>
> *Alack, alack!*
> *For the Church sake,*
> *Poor commons wake,*
> *And no marvel!*
> *For clear it is,*
> *The decay of this,*
> *How the poor shall miss*

No tongue can tell.

For there they had
Both ale and bread
At time of need,
And succour great
In all distress,
And heaviness,
And well entreat

In trouble and care,
Where that we were
In manner all bare
Of our substance,
We found good bate
At church men gate
Without checkmate
Or variance.

God, that right all,
Redress now shall,
And that is thrall
Again make free,
By this voyage
And pilgrimage
Of young and sage
In this country,

Whom God grant grace!
And for this space
Of this their trace,

Send them good speed,
With wealth, health and speed
Of sin's release,
And joy endless
When they be dead.

Church men forever
So you remember
Both first and later
In your memento
These pilgrims poor,
That take such cure
To stablish sure,
Which did undo

Crim, Cram, and Rich,
With three 'L' and the lich
As some men teach.
God them amend!
And that Aske may
Without delay
Here make a stay
And well to end!

IV

Melton was in a melancholy mood the next morning. He was worried about Harry, who had not shown up, and was even more worried about the dilapidated state of the castle.

"It's not got any better since you last looked at it," he said to Wyatt. "In short, it can hardly stand up, never mind stand a siege!"

"Well we'll have to see what we can do," said Wyatt in a no-nonsense tone. With the dawn he had set his emotions aside and become the man of action once again.

"How long have we got?" said Melton.

"Not long. The main army is waiting in Nottingham for my order to march."

'Where will we put them?"

"In the outer bailey, as I said. We will organise working parties to start today. I want a new palisade put up at once. The pilgrims are massing at Pontefract. 30,000 of them, I've heard, so there is no time to lose. I want every able-bodied man in the town working on the palisade."

"But where will the wood come from?"

"The castle woods."

"But..."

"I know. It's your little investment. But don't worry. The king will compensate you."

"But who will do the work?"

"The townsfolk. Any man who resists will find himself our guest – in the dungeon. Tom, find Bosville and send him to me."

Melton added, "And find Hugh, too. I want him to get some stonemasons to see to the cracks in the south curtain."

Then he turned to Wyatt. "What about the keep?"

"We can use the Great Chamber, but I seem to remember that the floor of the Solar is not safe."

"It is rotted through."

"Well, lay planks where the guards must walk to get to the parapet, and clear any rubble from the roof. I've got something very special to put up there."

"What's that?"

"Two cannon. From that position they can command the valley road."

"They'll bring the place down."

"No, those walls will stand until kingdom come. It's carrying them up that I'm worried about."

"We could fix up a winch on the keep wall-walk. That way we'll not have to haul them across that rotten floor. I'll ask Hugh to see to it."

"As for the Great Chamber I want that renovated to its former magnificence. Put my bed in there, too, behind a screen. I will make it my quarters. If I have any negotiating to do, I will do it there, in the most impressive room in the castle."

"I'll see to it," said Hugh.

"What can I do, father?" said Tom.

"Practice at the pell. There'll be hot work before this thing is over, mark my words, and a bit of training might come in handy – oh, and keep away from that kitchen maid!"

Soon the castle was buzzing with activity as hundreds of labourers set about their chopping, sawing, hammering, chiselling, cementing and general repairing. Melton walked up and down, overseeing the work, and seeming almost to enjoy himself, and indeed it was a pleasure to him to see his beloved castle receive some much-needed repairs.

"Ah, if only we had time to do it properly!" he was heard to say. "We could build another bastion to support the south curtain. We could re-roof the keep and put a new floor in the solar."

Young Tom, who had preferred to do the rounds with him, rather than tire himself out at the pell, bit his lip for once and said nothing about artillery.

V

Harry woke early, shivering with cold and damp, but full of excitement. There was nothing for breakfast other than hard bread and cold water, but he didn't mind. He had never known luxury, though food and warmth had never been wanting in the castle kitchen. And anyway, news of the forthcoming conference took his mind off his stomach. Word was passed round that lords, knights, gentleman and commons were assembling from all parts of the north to discuss with the leader of the pilgrimage, Thomas Aske, what their demands should be.

Harry spent the rest of the morning with the Conisbrough men looking for food. Father Ermystead impressed upon them that they must on no account take anything without paying for it. This was a Christian pilgrimage, and they must uphold Christian values, or what was the point? Every man emptied his purse, and Harry took out his little store of coppers to put into the general fund. Then they set off into Pontefract to see what could be bought.

The pilgrims might have been trying to uphold Christian values, but the townsfolk knew when they were onto a good thing and were determined to make the most of it.

"What! Sixpence for that starveling porker! It's all skin and bone!" said Barley-O who was bargaining for a pig.

"Wiv 30,000 men eatin' us out o' 'ouse and 'ome, what can yer expec'?" said the stallholder, brazenly.

"I'll gi' yer thru'pence for it."

"Nay, if tha wain't pay sixpence, there's plen'y as will!"

Barley-O gave in and handed over the sixpence.

"Well, it's daylight robbery, that's what I say!"

"Call it what yer like – we've got to ate as well, an' by t' time you lot've finished there'll be nowt left!"

After a dozen similar encounters, the Conisbrough party had enough for a good dinner, and they had also bought several loaves of bread and some strips of dried meat to keep them going later.

"Ah 'ope it's not goin' ter be *jaw jaw* for days, or we're like ter starve!" said Barley-O

"Well, you know what these 'ere nobles are like when they get in a meetin'. They don't know when ter stop. They forget that poor folk like us 'ave got a livin' to mek," said Jack the Rabbit-Catcher.

Fortunately, by the end of the day, the nobles and commons had agreed ten demands to put to the king. At the command of the Duke of Norfolk, who was negotiating on the king's behalf, the demands were not to be shared with the army or the people, but rumour is like water in a leaky sieve, and the gist of the demands was soon known and circulated through the crowd: a return to Catholicism, a recognition of the Pope, and a request for the stifling of heresy and plunder. They also heard that the army was preparing to march on Doncaster on the following day.

THAT NIGHT, AS WYATT was sitting down at the high table in the Great Hall at Conisbrough Castle, a man hurried up to him and whispered something in his ear. He frowned as he listened, then turning to Melton, he said, "My messenger tells me that the pilgrims are going to march on Doncaster tomorrow. There is no time to lose. I must send for the garrison."

Melton was taken aback.

"But we are not ready!"

"Oh, never mind that. The work can go on while the men are settling in."

Then he turned back to his messenger and gave him instructions to ride to Nottingham where the garrison was waiting.

All this was done in a moment, and quietly, but the men in the hall seemed to sense that something was afoot and the atmosphere was charged with excitement. Men talked in louder voices, laughed raucously, and drank deeply.

"If they come here, it'll be like the Battle of Wakefield," said one of the men-at-arms.

"Why? What happened? Tell us about it?"

The man shook his head and said he didn't know much, except that the castle, with a small garrison to defend it, was surrounded by a huge army. Melton looked up with interest, listened for a while, then intervened to correct the speaker.

"It wasn't this castle, it was Sandal, but the Yorkists were led by the lord of this castle, Richard, Duke of York. The

Lancastrians, led by the Duke of Somerset, surrounded the castle with about 10,000 men..."

"10,000! I heard there's 30,000 or more at Pontefract!"

There was a chorus of loud groans from the men.

"The Duke of York's garrison was about 5,000..."

"5,000! – and we're to get 150!"

"At that time, the king had garrisoned Conisbrough with 200 men – not many more than we are to have. This is a strong castle – one of the strongest in England..."

"Was. It's falling down!"

"The Duke of York made the mistake of sallying forth to give battle. Nobody knows why. Perhaps he thought that Somerset had fewer men. Perhaps he was over-confident."

"Ah 'ope you're not thinkin' 'o sallying forth?" said a man-at-arms. The man, of course, was deep in his cups, or he would not have spoken so boldly to the seneschal of the castle. Serjeant Bosville looked hard at him, and made a mental note to give him a dressing down and extra duty when he was sober.

Wyatt intervened.

"King Henry's orders are clear: hold the castle, and 150 are quite enough to do that. With a garrison in this castle no army would dare to use Doncaster Road, or Strafford Ford."

"What happened at the Battle of Wakefield?"

Melton looked uncomfortable, but had no choice but to answer the question.

"Richard of York found himself hopelessly outnumbered, attempted a fighting retreat, but was overcome and killed not far from Sandal Castle."

There were more groans from the men.

Young Tom showed little interest in all this. After all, had not that battle been fought over 70 years ago, and had not the art of war made considerable advances since then? In any case, he was more interested in the art of love than the art of war, and was keeping an eye open for Sally. Unfortunately, Mrs Goodlad was also keeping an eye open for Sally – watching her every move, in fact, so Tom never caught so much as a glimpse of her that evening.

BY NOON NEXT DAY, MRS Goodlad had something else to worry about.

"Well, I never! Here I am a skivvy in my own kitchen! Me lord's cook's just moved in and took o'er, an' ah'm ter fetch an' carry as though ah'd nivver cooked a dinner in me life!"

"Well, I like it," said Sally. "It's nice ter see a bit o' life in the ol' place."

"I know what yer mean by 'life', yer brazen 'ussy. You mean them men-at-arms!"

"Only t' other day ye were encouragin' me to," protested Sally.

"Proper courtin' ah were talkin' about! Norra quick 'un behind t' buttress. Mark my words, young lady, ah s'll be watchin' thee like a 'awk!"

Just then, the garrison head cook came over to them.

"You two can help in the field kitchen in the Outer Bailey."

"Yes, sir," they chorused with a respectful bob, but as soon as he had gone, Mrs Goodlad started complaining.

"Well, ah nivver! Ah'm not even allowed ter skivvy in my own kitchen, but ah'm sent to work in a tent in a field!"

"Come on, mam. Let's get on wi' it."

KNIGHTS AND THEIR SQUIRES, and serjeants-at-arms, were to be quartered in the Inner Bailey, while the men-at arms, archers, fletchers, farriers, blacksmiths and assorted varlets were to be quartered in the outer bailey in leather tents. The largest tent of all was the field kitchen to which Mrs Goodlad and Sally had been sent.

All afternoon the serjeants-at-arms were marching up and down and shouting orders to their men in an attempt to get the castle on a defensive footing as soon as possible.

Hugh found himself in charge of the Castlegardurn men, all of whom were very much surprised to find themselves with a helmet on their head and a halberd in their hand. They knew that they had to pay the Castlegardurn tax, but few knew why, because it was an ancient feudal obligation that was all but forgotten. They held their lands in return for military service, and paid tax in lieu of it. However, their lord could summon them to serve in person in times of need, and Wyatt, believing that every man would count, had invoked the ancient law. These were old Conisbrough families, some of whom had already been in Conisbrough for hundreds of years before Seigneur Varenne usurped the Honour of Conisbrough, which had belonged to good King Harold before the Conquest. Let me rehearse a few of them:

Appleyard, Battie, Booth, Bosville, Brocklesby, Brownell, Cowley, Ellershaw, Dufton, Greathead, Hurst, Mason, Oldham, Webster, Westby.

They were the most unmilitary rabble you could imagine: fat burghers whose pot bellies bulged out under their breastplates, scrawny youths who could hardly stand up in their armour, old men dragged from their firesides. In short, a 16th century Dad's army.

Hugh did his best to lick them into shape, but they were only fit for the humblest of jobs, which was to police the civilians in the castle – the small army of fletchers, farriers, blacksmiths and varlets – thus allowing the real men-at-arms to focus on military matters.

As night fell, twenty men were on guard at various points around the castle, more than had been on guard at any time since the Battle of Wakefield, and though the repairs were still in progress, the castle was secure enough. Which is just as well, because a messenger from the king's representative, the Duke of Norfolk, arrived to announce that the rebels, as he called them, were encamped outside Doncaster.

VI

I t was noon before the pilgrims got started and they made slow progress. The army marched first, followed by the baggage train, and the non-combatant civilians brought up the rear.

They had not been on the march long when Barley-O said, "Why're we guin' this way? It's quicker to gu dahn't Don Valley."

"And what guards the Don Valley?" said Harry, with a touch of pride. "Conisbrough Castle – that's what! Wi' a garrison at Conisbrough Castle, Aske daren't expose our flank."

"But it's no good approaching Donny from t' north. Norfolk's bound ter 'old North Bridge."

"There's a ford, in't there?"

"Aye, but not a good 'un. It don't tek much ter flood it aht!"

Hearing their despondent talk, Father Ermystead did what he could to cheer them up:

"Come on, lads, let's sing the Pilgrim's Hymn to help us on our way!"

Christ crucified!
For thy wounds wide,
Us commons guide!

Which pilgrims be,
Through God's grace,
For to purchase
Old wealth and peace
Of the spirituality.

By the time they reached Doncaster, it was getting dark, and they made camp to the north of the town. Harry slept uneasily that night. He'd had nothing but a bit of bread to eat, and was so far from the fire, that he felt he was going to freeze to death. But that was nothing to his fears for the next day. The sight of the huge army – now numbering about 40,000 men – and their arms and armour had made a big impression on him. He was expecting a great battle, and believed that he would be expected to play a part in it – though with what, he couldn't guess, because he had nothing more than the small table knife which he used to cut his food.

He woke before dawn, and stood shivering under a tree, looking through the darkness towards Doncaster, but with the army strung out along the road, it was miles away from where he was standing.

At last black night paled to a grey, drizzly dawn. All around him people were waking up, wet cold and dispirited. He hoped that the men of the army were in better heart. Barley-O tried to light a fire, but all the wood was wet. Nor was there anything left to eat. So they sat down under the tree and waited for something to happen.

The rain stopped and the day brightened, but Harry's stomach still complained.

"Ah've 'ad enough 'o this," said Barley-O. "Ah'm guin' ter try ter find summat ter ate. Ar't' comin'?"

Harry was just about to follow him, when news came from the front line.

"What is it?" said Harry.

"They say that t' Duke o' Norfolk's on'y got 5,000 men."

"That's good isn't it?" said Harry.

"Aye, but he's got artillery."

"Artillery?"

"Aye. It's the modern world come to blow thy brains out. He's 'oldin' North Bridge wi' a battery o' cannon, so our leader, Aske, can't do owt. We've got 40,000 men but not one cannon among us."

"What about the ford?"

"Wi' all this rain, it's flooded."

Tom felt a sudden sense of frustration. Was this it? Were the high ideal of the Pilgrimage of Grace and its early successes at York and Pontefract to end at North Bridge because of a swollen river and a few cannon? He paced up and down, his mind racing.

"Well, ah'm gunna find summat to ate, an' then ah'm off 'ome," said Barley-O. "Ah'm not stopping 'ere wi' cannon balls flyin' arahnd! Tha comin?"

Tom shook his head, hardly hearing what Barley-O had said, and continued to pace. Then he had an idea – Strafford Ford. Strafford Ford was a ford between Conisbrough and Mexborough which was always easy to cross, rain or no rain. He would tell Aske about Strafford Ford and then the army could cross the river and approach Doncaster from the west, outflanking Norfolk's cannon. He hurried to tell Father

Ermystead, but stopped in his tracks – he would be betraying Conisbrough – the castle which had been his home all his life. He would be putting his adopted family at risk. Poor old, overweight Hugh might find himself crossing swords with a fit, strong knight – but then, the Pilgrimage! The Monks who had taken him in when nobody wanted him! Religion! Christ crucified! Those words brought a verse of the Pilgrim's Hymn to mind:

> *God, that rights all,*
> *Redress now shall,*
> *And that is thrall*
> *Again make free,*
> *By this voyage*
> *And pilgrimage*
> *Of young and sage*
> *In this country.*

Yes, God would right all. He would tell Father Ermystead. That decided, he hurried off to find him.

Father Ermystead listened with growing interest as Harry told him what he had thought of. He didn't expect such a young, uneducated man to know anything about military strategy, but soon realised that he had underestimated him.

"Harry," he said solemnly. "I think you may well be right. Come with me. We will get word to Aske somehow."

It was not easy. First they had to find him in the confusing deployments of rank upon rank of armed men, and then they had to get permission to see him. Harry could never have done it alone, and even Father Ermystead's clerical habit was no automatic passport. But at last Father Ermystead was able to tell their leader Harry's idea, giving credit where it was due, though Harry had found himself tongue-tied in the presence of the great man.

Aske responded quickly, turning to Lord Scrope of Bolton, his second-in-command.

"Take half the men..." then he turned to Harry.

"Do you know the quickest way from here?"

Harry said that he did.

"And the way from the ford to Doncaster."

"Aye but..."

"What is it, young man?"

"They'll 'ave to pass Conisbrough Castle, an' ah 'eard that it was to 'ave a big garrison."

"How big?"

"I 'eard 150, sire."

Aske laughed. "We will outnumber them ten to one. Scrope, peel off 5,000 men to surround the castle. That will make sure they don't harass our flanks."

Several details were thrashed out, and then Scrope, signalling Harry to follow him, left Aske's tent to carry out his orders. Tom's heart sank. It was too late to back out now. He hoped – prayed – he had done the right thing, and that Hugh and his family would not suffer because of it.

VII

Hugh was in the guard house warming himself by the fire, taking advantage of the fact that William Webster and George Booth, Castlegardurn men, could do his most disliked duty – night watch on the lookout tower, the thin high tower that overlooks the barbican.

The watch was nearly over, and chill night was beginning to turn into a misty dawn, when young William came bustling through the door of the guardhouse.

"There's armed men outside!"

Hugh jumped to his feet and shook the shoulders of the dozing men-at-arms on either side of him.

"Many?"

"'Undreds, sarge!"

A moment later, another guard – one of Wyatt's men – ran though the door.

"Armed men outside the Outer Gatehouse!"

At the same time, the alarm bell started ringing, and soon there were men running everywhere. Hugh decided to climb to the top of the lookout tower where he would have the best view.

He arrived puffing and panting after having dragged his overweight body up several flights of steps. George was staring down through an embrasure with such shocked absorption that he didn't notice his master's noisy arrival. Hugh went to another embrasure and looked down. It was early and the light was dim, and a damp fog lingered in castle ditch, but it was not difficult to make out the shapes of armed men creeping up towards the castle walls. Hearing the castle's alarm bell, they ceased the attempt to hide themselves, and marched boldly up to the castle walls.

Hugh's eyes nearly popped out of his head. "'undreds? – Thahsands, more like!" he muttered to himself, and immediately headed for the steps so that he could report to Melton.

But Melton and Wyatt had already received the news, and other news from the lookout at the top of the keep, that a large army was marching along the Don Valley road. They had hurried to the Outer Gatehouse to parley with their attackers, led by Lord Conyers, whom Lord Scrope had delegated to surround the castle.

"Open your gates and surrender," demanded Lord Conyers. "I give you my word that no-one will be harmed. We are Christian pilgrims and wish to avoid bloodshed."

"You are rebels," said Wyatt bluntly, "and we hold this castle in the king's name."

"Mightier places than this have fallen!" scoffed Conyers. "Hull, York, Pontefract."

Wyatt realised that this kind of talk could only lead one way – to battle, and that was not what he wanted. Conisbrough was strongly garrisoned, but the castle was nowhere near as strong as it was in former times. The whole of the south curtain was tottering, and the outer bailey, where he now stood, was a hastily erected wooden construction, far inferior to the stone outer bailey that had crumbled away many years ago. The messenger of the night before had told him that the Duke of Norfolk's plan was to keep the rebels talking until a relief army arrived. He must do the same.

"Come," said Wyatt. "We are both gentlemen and it is unseemly to bandy words in front of our inferiors. I will grant you safe passage if you will agree a truce, and honour me by a visit to my private chamber."

Conyers exchanged a few words with his second in command, Lord Darcy, and then agreed to the truce.

"One more thing," said Wyatt. "The king commanded me to defend the Don Valley, so you must send a message to your main army to halt its advance."

Conyers laughed – a great, disdainful guffaw.

"How many men have you here? Enough to stop an army of 20,000? I don't think so."

Wyatt responded with a confident smile. "Not so many men, perhaps, but we have something else..."

He waved a signal to a man-at-arms on the top of the keep. Moments later a tremendous roar echoed through the Don Valley.

"...a battery of cannon on top of the keep – which is the perfect position to command the valley. Don't worry about your friends – that was a warning shot."

Wyatt, the poet, was playing with words. 'Battery' means a group. Strictly speaking it is the correct term for any group of cannons where there is more than one, though the word implies several. Wyatt was not lying. There was more than one cannon on top of the keep, but only one more. Two cannons, even though most advantageously positioned, could not stop an army of 20,000.

But it was enough to wipe the arrogant expression off Conyer's face. Again, he conferred with Darcy, and again he gave his agreement. Moments later, a messenger was galloping to Lord Scrope to tell him the news that he was covered by a battery of cannon and should halt immediately. The negotiations being concluded, Wyatt ordered the gates to be opened to admit Lord Conyers and Lord Darcy and two attendant squires. Harry, who had been watching all this from a distance, breathed a sigh of relief. There was not going to be any fighting – at least, not yet.

Wyatt led the visitors to the castle keep, up the steps, over the drawbridge, and up the wide, winding staircase to the Great Chamber. He noted with satisfaction that his renovations were having the desired effect. The Great Chamber in Conisbrough Castle keep is not large, but it is impressive. Not only can you sense the thickness of the walls, which are fifteen foot thick at their widest, but you can see it in the window seat, which is, in effect, a room cut out of the thickness of the wall, with a huge double window overlooking the bailey. The hooded fireplace is equally impressive, especially with the royal arms displayed on a large escutcheon placed above it. Those arms spoke in no uncertain terms of the power of the king of England.

One side of the chamber was screened off for a bed – the solar above being uninhabitable because of the state of the roof, and on the other side was a small round table, where Wyatt invited his guests to sit. On the wall nearby was a tapestry depicting the knights of King Arthur seated at their round table. This was Melton's idea. He had moved the tapestry from the Great Hall to replace the rotting tapestry in the Great Chamber, in the hope of reminding visitors of Conisbrough's illustrious history, for legend tells that, long ago, Conisbrough was Camelot, and it was here that the celebrated King Arthur held his court.

Wyatt sent for wine, and the negotiations began.

"Join us," said Lord Conyers, "in support of the true faith."

Melton gave a little laugh and said, "Gentlemen, you do not know your man. Wyatt, here, has a family tradition of unbending loyalty."

Then he went on to give a brief account of the senior Wyatt's loyalty under imprisonment and torture, and did not forget to add a few words about the loyalty that had recently earned Sir Thomas his knighthood.

Conyers, visibly impressed, took a deep draught of wine, and said, "I, too value loyalty. I am loyal to the Pope and the true church."

"I respect that too," said Melton with rather too much enthusiasm.

Wyatt said nothing, but was probably thinking that loyalty was a complicated matter.

"Then we are not far from agreement," said Conyers.

"I don't see how we can reach agreement," said Wyatt, "but we certainly understand each other."

"Join us!" urged Conyers again. "With you on our side, we hold the Don Valley and can take Doncaster. Then the king must listen."

"150 more fighting men can make no difference," said Wyatt. "Nor does it make much difference whether I hold up your army or not. You still have 20,000 men at Doncaster against the Duke of Norfolk's 5,000, and from what I have heard the outcome will not be decided by fighting, but by negotiation."

"That is true, said Conyers. "Even as we talk, our leader, Aske, is negotiating a settlement.

"Then I invite all the nobles and gentlefolk among you to join us at a feast in the Great Hall tonight. We will agree to differ, gentlemen, and we need not fight."

VIII

Of course, the great folk needed their squires and servants, and that is how Harry managed to get into the castle. He hoped he could slip back unnoticed to his tiny bed space under the tiles of the kitchen roof, and then slip unobtrusively back into his usual duties, as though he had never been away. But Hugh's eagle eyes spotted him before he was halfway across the bailey.

"Arrest that man!" he snapped.

William Webster was the recipient of the order, but he had never arrested anybody in his life, and had no idea what to do. Hugh told him.

"Disarm 'im, bind 'is hands, an' throw him in t' dungeon."

William approached Harry cautiously, but Harry had no thought of resisting – except with words.

"Why? What 'ave ah done?"

"Betrayed Conisbrough, that's what! Fightin' in t' rebel army."

"But nobody's fighting – an' anyway, we're pilgrims."

"Pilgrims, my arse! Pilgrims wi' swords and spears an' a dunno know what else!" Then, turning to the still hesitating William, "Gu on. Tek 'im to t' dungeon."

"But there's rats dahn theer!" objected Harry.

"Aye and tha'll be t' biggest on 'em all!"

That night at the feast in the Great Hall, Melton was happier than ever before. Surely this was the greatest gathering of England's nobility to be seen at Conisbrough Castle ever – or at least since the days of the De Warennes. Wyatt was also happy – or, at least, content. He was still too heartsore about the events at the Tower to be happy. But he was pleased that his poet's way with words had soothed his attackers and avoided a siege. All they had to do now was await the outcome of the negotiations in Doncaster.

The knights and men-at-arms of both sides were happy too. The hosts, because many of them had a secret sympathy with the cause of their guests, and the guests because they were eating and drinking their fill instead of spilling each other's blood.

Due to a shortage of pages, Sally had managed to escape skivvying in the field kitchen and insinuated herself among the serving staff in the castle kitchen.

She was glad that Harry was back, and not unduly concerned that he had been thrown in the dungeon, for she was confident that she could talk her father round and get him released. In the meantime, she intended to enjoy herself. She put on her lowest gown, taking advantage of the fact that her mother was not around to tell her off, and spent the evening serving wine and flirting with the knights, not forgetting to give special attention to her particular fancy, young Tom.

At the same time, a much bigger feast was taking place in the Outer Bailey on trestle tables set up in the open. Here were all the men-at-arms, fletchers, farriers, blacksmiths and even the Castlegardurn men who sat at the least privileged table near the gate and far from the kitchen. This meant that they were served last, and constantly interrupted by comings and goings at the gate. Wyatt had wisely forbidden any men, other than the nobility, from entering the castle, but that didn't stop a lot of friendly trade, especially as the men outside had money to spend, and the castle was well-stocked with provisions.

The only men who were not present at the feast were those on guard duty. This included eighteen of the king's men-at-arms, and the two Castlegardurn men who were on night duty, William and George.

George was stationed on the south bastion, which was safe enough, despite the state of the adjacent curtain walls, but which rumour had caused him to worry about. However, William had the worse of it. He was on the lookout tower, and not only had he a panoramic view of the festivities, he was tormented by the exquisite aroma of roasted meat.

Down in the Outer Bailey the rest of the Castlegardurn men were enjoying themselves for once.

"This beats a farmer's life!" said Westby taking a deep draught of ale.

"That it do!" agreed Battie. "Ah were up at t' crack o' dawn, muckin' aht t' pigs, an' feedin' t' chickens. Then ah were in't top field mekkin' them lazy peasants do a bit o' wuk fur a change…"

"It's not all feastin' yer know, bein' a man-at-arms," said Hugh. "Nah, if it an't a been for my maister's clever words, it'd be like a slaughter 'ouse rahd 'ere!"

"Nah, not in these times," said Greathead. "An Englishman will not fight an Englishman – we'll save fightin' for t' Frogs an' t' Jocks!"

"Well, t' only thing ah'm stickin' is this pig on me plate," said Battie. "Bring more ale, ho!"

Mrs Goodlad answered the call. She plonked down the pitcher so sharply that the table wobbled, and the ale slopped over the top. She was clearly in a bad mood.

"What is it, my love?" said Hugh.

"It's all reet for thee to sit there eatin' an' drinkin' while ah'm slaving in that tent, an' somebody else is mussing up my kitchin – an' another thing. Where's our Sally? She's supposed ter be lookin' after Totty, but ah'll bet she's 'angin' rahnd the young maister again. Nah, get thy lazy arse off that bench an' gu an' find 'er afore she gets up stick!"

With that, Mrs Goodlad stormed off back to the kitchen and the Castlegardurn men indulged in a little laughter at Hugh's expense. Only a little, mind you, for most of them were not strangers to similar tongue-lashings.

"Got to go, lads. Now, mark you, Westby and Greathead, you're on fust watch. Don't drink too much and oversleep or ah'll s'll 'ave yer in't dungeon to keep 'Arry company!"

Having thus asserted his authority and quelled the laughter, Hugh stamped off, somewhat unsteadily, to find his wayward daughter. He headed for the most likely place – that corner between the north-east buttress of the keep and the curtain wall, but word must have preceded him, for all he found was his daughter walking towards the kitchen, and no sign of Tom. However, she was heading away from the keep corner, and her clothing seemed rather rumpled. Hugh grabbed her by the wrist and gave her a few sharp words:

"Nah, then, thou brazen hussy, what hast tha been up to this time?"

"Nothin' dad. It were a call o' nature."

"What's up wi' t' garderobe, then? 'Ere we are in a castle wiv every modern convenience, and you gu behind a buttress!"

"Wi' fifty knights drinkin' their fill, what do yer expect? They's all occupied an' ah couldn't wait"

"Well, then, tha's better get thysen to t' field kitchen where yer mam can keep an eye on yer. Better still, I'll tek thee mesen!"

Actually, Hugh was wrong about his daughter. She had not been frolicking with young Tom behind the buttress, though what she had been doing might have angered him even more. She had been up the steps to the keep, charmed the guard, passed over the drawbridge, and lowered a bundle of food to Harry in the dungeon, who as a result of his bold expedition had risen in her estimation from a nobody to somebody worth a girl's admiration.

IX

Things continued in the same way for the next few days, then on Thursday afternoon there was news from Doncaster. A messenger from the Duke of Norfolk had brought a message to Lord Scrope and Lord Conyers to say that an agreement had been reached between Aske on behalf of the pilgrims, and Norfolk on behalf of the king. Wyatt invited Melton, Conyers and Darcy to the Great Chamber of the keep to discuss the settlement.

"These were the demands of the pilgrims," said Conyers, reading from a paper:

> *(1) That a general pardon should be granted, without any exceptions;*

> *(2) That a parliament should be held at York or Nottingham, or some other convenient place;*

> *(3) That no man residing north of the Trent should be compelled, by subpœna, to attend any court except York, unless in matters of allegiance;*

> *(4) That some Acts of the late Parliament, which were too grievous to the people, should be repealed;*

(6) That the Princess Mary should be declared legitimate;

(6) That the suppressed monasteries should be restored to their former state;

(7) That the Papal Authority should be re-established;

(8) That heretical books should be suppressed, and heretics punished according to law;

(9) That Lord Cromwell, the vicar-general, Lord Audley, the chancellor, and Rich, the attorney-general, should be removed from the Council; and

(10) That Leigh and Layton, visitors of the northern monasteries, should be prosecuted for their briberies and extortions.

"The duke replied on behalf of the king that if the insurgents would return to their homes, the royal mercy would be extended to all the rebels, and a promise given that their grievances should be discussed in a parliament which should be held at York."

Lord Darcy frowned and shook his head doubtfully, but Melton and Wyatt smiled, looked at each other, and nodded their satisfaction at the happy outcome.

"Aske has agreed to disperse his troops, so we will depart too. I will trespass on your hospitality for one more night, but by this time tomorrow, we will be gone."

"Tonight we will celebrate," said Wyatt, "because, in a way, we are both winners. I have been loyal to the king and held Conisbrough in his name, and you have won a hearing in parliament."

"Yes," said Lord Conyers. "It is a kind of victory – and with not a drop of blood being spilled, but…"

Darcy continued for him, "Will it make any difference? Once our army is dispersed we are at the king's mercy."

Wyatt tried to reassure him. "Come, now, Darcy. I have often been at court, and the king is an honourable man."

But it was his loyalty speaking, not his true self. He knew too well the king's perfidy. Had he not he spent months in prison without having committed a crime? Had he not seen his lover executed at the king's word, even though she was innocent? But he said nothing of this, being glad enough to have survived a testing time and come through with honour.

That night saw the most uproarious celebration that the castle had ever known, but by noon, next day, the place was as silent as the crypt in Conisbrough Church. The rebels had gone home, the king's men had marched back to Nottingham, and even the Castlegardurn men had returned to their farms.

They had many a tall tale to tell in the years to come of the days of their military service. The peaceful investment of the castle turned into a mighty siege of which each Castlegardurn man was the hero, and the more years that passed the taller the tales grew, as there were fewer and fewer to remember that not a single life was lost, though many a butt of ale was drained.

The following day, a messenger came from the king. Wyatt frowned as he read the message.

"Melton," he said. "I must leave, and that soon. "I have been given a new mission – the king's Ambassador to Spain."

"Another reward for your loyalty?"

"Indeed," said Wyatt, "though to be honest, I'd rather stay in England. My wife is with child, and my son is about to be married."

By 'wife', Melton understood him to be referring to his Mistress, Elizabeth Darrel, but the news of his son's betrothal came as a complete surprise – especially considering his behaviour towards Sally. But then, he reasoned, it was probably a marriage of convenience – nothing that would interfere with a young aristocrat's *amours*. Nevertheless, he made a mental note to let Hugh know about it, as it might help to keep Sally out of trouble.

"I am glad of it," said Melton at last, "but what of Conisbrough?"

"I retain my post as constable, but there is little enough to be done here. You must return the castle to its peacetime footing, and I will visit you once in a while."

"Very well, it shall be done," said Melton. I shall be sorry to see the old place neglected again, but at least I saw the castle in one of its moments of glory."

"You are right," said Wyatt. "We have witnessed one of the castle's great moments. Perhaps I shall write a poem about it."

Melton, looking at his friend, saw that his features had softened. He was no longer the hard-faced man of action, but a gentle-hearted poet once again. Also, it seemed that the stirring events of the recent conflict had put a distance between Wyatt and his grief. He was happy for his friend, but nearly forgot a little detail that needed attending to.

"Before you go, my lord, I have one more favour to ask. It is the matter of Harry who is in the dungeon awaiting your judgement."

"Send him to me," said Wyatt. "He will find me in the Great Chamber."

Perhaps the scene that follows was the last significant episode in the history of the Great Chamber. It had been pulled back from near ruin by the rebellion, but from that day onward would receive not a single hammer blow of maintenance.

Wyatt sat at the round table in front of the King Arthur tapestry. It was an imposing sight for poor Harry who was not sure whether he was going to be sent back to the dungeon or hanged, drawn and quartered. He stood, shivering with fright, staring at his dirty, naked feet.

"Tell me why you betrayed the king, Harry."

Put like that, it sounded a terrible crime, and poor Harry could hardly find a voice to speak with, but he managed to explain to Wyatt how the monks of Roche Abbey had taken him in when he was abandoned as a baby, and how he felt that his first loyalty was to them and their religion.

The word 'loyalty' struck a sympathetic chord in Wyatt, not that he was ill-disposed to the young man.

"Harry, listen carefully," he said. "I understand what you did. But you are a son of Conisbrough now, and your loyalty should be to this castle, to Melton as your seneschal, to me as your constable, and above all to the king, who is lord of this castle. And loyalty is not conditional. My motto, as you may know, is *loyaulte me lie*... but I am forgetting myself, you know no Latin. It means..."

Harry interrupted him. "I know a little, my lord, once again, thanks to the monks. Your motto means 'loyalty binds me'."

Wyatt looked at the young man with surprise. "I am impressed, Harry. There is more about you than I realised. But listen, it is the 'binding' part of the motto that is important. Your loyalty should bind you, even at times when you don't want to be loyal, even when you disagree with your master, and you want to rebel. I have been loyal to the king, through – I will not tell you what difficulties – and he has rewarded me. First with a knighthood and two constableships, and now – I will say no more at the moment, but you will hear of it."

Harry looked at his feet and said nothing.

"I shall be watching you, young Harry, and if you prove to be loyal in the times to come – for this matter of the pilgrimage is not resolved yet – I will see to it personally that you are rewarded. Now, you are free to go and to resume your normal duties in the stable. I will speak to your master, and to Mr and Mrs Goodlad, so that they know what I have said to you."

Harry couldn't believe his luck and hurried from the Great Chamber as fast as his feet would carry him without actually running.

PART 4:

"And I myself, myself always to hate."

I

Wyatt's mission to Spain was even more unpleasant than he expected. His 'diet', or allowance, was nowhere hear enough to cover his costs, and he found that he was having to keep himself out of his own pocket. If that wasn't bad enough, the mission itself was almost impossible. He had been charged with preventing an alliance between Catholic France and Catholic Spain – but what could one man do? His main opponent was a man called Reginald Pole. Pole had been King Henry's protegee, and was well on the way to becoming the next Archbishop of Canterbury. However, when he failed to support him in the matter of the divorce he was hounded out of the kingdom. Pole resolved to be revenged on Henry, and what better way than to unite the kings of Catholic Christendom against him? For months Wyatt tried every diplomatic means he could think of – and he was no mean diplomat. As a poet gifted in the nuances of language, and able to speak both French and Spanish, he was capable of much – but the task was simply too great. In the end, in a kind of mad despair, he announced that, since diplomacy had failed, he would find Pole and have him murdered. Surprisingly, this tactic worked, for Pole fled the Spanish court, lingered for a while in Paris, but, hearing that Wyatt was pursuing him, didn't stay long. In the meantime, Wyatt secretly returned to England.

Thus his mission was a success, though in an unexpected way. What was even more unexpected was his arrest not long after. He was thrown into prison on the basis of a letter from Bishop Bonner to the king, accusing Wyatt of conspiring with Pole – it was nonsense, of course, but in those dangerous days even the faintest suspicion was enough to condemn a man.

So it was that Wyatt found himself in prison once again – and not a comfortable gentleman's prison this time. His friends at court had gone or deserted him. His father was dead, and even Cromwell had been executed. As a result, he was put in a common dungeon in the Tower. He had few comforts, though he did manage to get hold of pen and parchment, and was able to write letters to those who thought might help him, and this poem to his old friend Sir Francis Bryan:

> *Sighs are my food, my drink are my tears;*
> *Clinking of fetters would such music crave;*
> *Stink, and close air away my life it wears;*
> *Poor innocence is all the hope I have:*
> *Rain, wind, or weather judge I by my ears:*
> *Malice assaults, that righteousness should have.*
> *Sure am I, Bryan, this wound shall heal again,*

But yet, alas, the scar shall still remain.

But he was not really sure. Bryan could do nothing to help, and none of his other letters bore fruit. Help, when it came, was from a most unexpected quarter – Henry Howard, Earl of Surrey. Wyatt knew Surrey as one of the wealthiest men in England, an arrogant popinjay who aspired to outshine him as court poet. Yet Surrey saw Wyatt as his a shining example of what a poet could achieve, and had come to revere him as a student reveres his master. Thus, one day, the prison door opened and Wyatt was set free as suddenly and unexpectedly as he had found himself a prisoner.

II

After his return, Harry's star seemed to rise suddenly. Before, it was as though he had been invisible, now, it seemed that everybody wanted to know him. Hugh spoke kindly to him, Mrs Goodlad gave him extra helpings at dinner, and even Sally was not too proud to smile at him. Most important of all for Harry was that Melton, at Brother Boniface's request, asked around in Conisbrough, and, for a small consideration, managed to place him as the blacksmith's apprentice. He didn't care for the work at first. It was very physical, hot and dangerous, but there was a good proportion of horse work which made the rest of it bearable.

The hard physical work of hammering and shaping that most recalcitrant of materials, along with the good dinners cooked by Mrs Smith, and served by Susan, the blacksmith's pretty daughter, soon filled out his gawky frame, and though he only earned a few coppers as an apprentice, it was enough to kit him out in a leather jerkin and new hose.

Harry sometimes came to the castle to shoe the horses in the castle stables, and of course, Sally was not slow to seek him out. She could hardly believe that he was the same gawky lad that had asked her to be his sweetheart a few years ago. His muscular frame and well-fitting clothes were only part of the transformation; his independence of mind in going on the pilgrimage, and his determination to get on had given him a new confidence. And if all that wasn't enough to make him desirable in her eyes, there was always the thought of Susan. She felt sure that that scheming hussy had her eyes on Harry – after all, what match could be more suitable?

"'Ello, 'Arry," she said, peering round the stable door.

"Oh, 'ello, Sally," said Harry, carrying on with his work. Indeed, he could hardly stop at that point, for he had Dobbin's hind leg between his knees and was hammering a horseshoe into place.

"'Ow's things at t' forge?" she said, trying to make conversation.

"All reet. 'Ow's things at t' castle."

"Borin' now you're not 'ere," said Sally, taking a chance.

Harry drove the last nail home and put down Dobbin's leg. Then he turned round, looked at Sally and gave a light laugh.

"What d' yer mean? Ah never got a chance to speak to yer. Yer were allus too busy for me."

Sally frowned.

"Ah suppose that Susan's got plenty of time for yer..." she hazarded.

"Mrs Smith and Susan take good care of me."

Suddenly Sally threw discretion to the winds, and said in an outburst of passion: "Ah'll tek care o' you better than 'er, any day. Just you try me!"

But now it was Harry's turn to play hard to get – though to be fair to him, he wasn't playing. He knew that Susan liked him, and he knew that the blacksmith had an eye on him as a future son-in-law. Of course, he preferred Sally. He had always liked her – loved her, even – but in those days, love was reserved for ballads and jongleur's songs. A knight married for land, a burgher married for a business, and by the same token, he felt it behoved him to marry for a smithy. He was no longer Harry, the gawky stable lad, he was Harry the apprentice blacksmith with coins in his pocket and prospects to look forward to. It was gratifying to have won Sally's love, but after all, she was only a kitchen maid and had nothing to offer. He decided that he would think about it.

"Well, ah must get on," he said. "Ah've got Bramble to do, and then ah've got to be getting back to t' forge."

"Aye, an' Susan!" said Sally, storming off in a huff.

Truth be told, Harry had other things to worry about, beside which any thoughts of sweethearts seemed trivial. Not long after the Pilgrims had dispersed, the king went back on his word to Aske. He said that he thought it strange that the pilgrims – whom he called 'brutes and inexpert folk' should meddle in affairs of state, and never did hold that parliament he promised. Instead, he had the rebel leaders, including Scrope, Conyers and Darcy, beheaded, and Aske was carried to York to be hanged in chains till he died. What was worse, many ordinary people were hanged in their own gardens as examples to their fellow villagers, and monks of Swaley Abbey, a suppressed monastery which the Pilgrims had re-established, were hanged from the steeple of their church.

As a result, a second uprising was begun in Cumberland and Westmoreland, and was spreading to Yorkshire. Harry was sorely tempted to join it, but he remembered his promise to Sir Thomas, and struggled to be loyal to him, the seneschal, the castle – and the king.

He would have gone to Father Ermystead for advice, but he had been replaced by a new man who was a Protestant and loyal to the king, so he set off to Roche to speak to his old mentor.

He found a scene of chaos. The King's Commissioners had had just received the 'voluntary' surrender of Roche Abbey, and the 17 monks had been sent away, each with a small pension and the contents of his cell. Crowds had already gathered in the hope of rich pickings, so it was difficult for Harry to find Brother Boniface. Eventually, however, he found a monk, who directed him to another monk, who pointed to a solitary figure walking along the road that led to Bawtry. Harry caught up with him and found him walking in along in a kind of daze as though he had no idea where he had come from and where he was going to.

"Brother Boniface!" he said, "It's me, Harry."

Brother Boniface shook his head.

"Not, 'Brother', no – for I am a monk no longer. Call me by my old name, William – Bill, for short."

"Where are you going?"

"Going?"

Bill's forehead crinkled as though this was the hardest theological conundrum that he had ever been tasked to solve. Then, looking ahead, and recognising a farm house, said, "Bawtry."

"Why Bawtry?" asked Harry.

"It's where I used to live – but heaven knows if there'll be anybody there now. My parents are long dead and my brother went to live in Nottingham."

"What will you live on?"

Bill gave a bitter laugh.

"The commissioners said we could keep the contents of our cells. But don't they know that a monk has nothing? I sold my spare robe for a ha'penny, but nobody would give me so much as a farthing for my poor pallet bed. I even tried to sell my door. It was a fine piece of oak with good iron fittings and worth tuppence, but they just laughed at me: 'why should we pay good coin when there's any amount of timber we can have for nothing?' they said, and they were right, for the king's commissioners allowed them to strip the place. It would have pitied any heart to see what tearing up of the lead there was, and plucking up of boards, and throwing down of the rafters. Everything was either spoiled, plucked away or defaced to the uttermost."

"I'm sorry to hear it," said Harry. "Why did you not resist?"

"And be hanged from our own steeple like the monks of Swaley? No. Abbot Henry said that we must accept the judgement as it came from the king – and perhaps from God. Did I not once say that the abbey had become too rich? Do you think the king would have bothered us if we had lived in a thatched hut in the middle of a muddy field?"

Bill looked at Harry to see how his words had been received, and seeing his face flushing red with anger, was quick to add a warning:

"Accept it, Harry, as I have to. Don't let your anger turn you from the path you have been following. You have stayed loyal to the castle. You have worked hard. Soon you will have your own smithy and a wife. There is nothing you can do here. My advice is to go home by another way and forget all about it."

"But what about you?"

Bill gave a weak smile.

"Don't worry about me. I will carry on teaching as before. It will be *amo, amas, amat* just like it always was..."

He paused as he reflected on it, then added, "but there will no help for waifs and strays like you were, Harry. No doubt I will be able to find places for a few poor scholars, but I will not have the funds to feed and clothe orphans."

"Let me know where you set up your school," said Harry, "and I will make sure to visit you."

"I will," said Bill, beginning to feel a little more optimistic about the future. "So goodbye for now. *Pax vobiscum...* ha ha ha... it will take me a long time to get out of my monkish habits."

Bill looked at his cassock and laughed again.

"Not to mention *this* habit!"

III

It was in summer of that year that Wyatt once again found himself on the road to Conisbrough. The first thing he noticed was that the wooden wall of the outer bailey, the construction of which he had himself supervised, was gone. The next thing was the huge gap in the castle where the south curtain wall had tumbled into the ditch. In the place where gatehouse of the Outer Bailey used to be was a small manor house built in the modern style with two storeys and small, mullioned windows. He stopped to enquire at the house, and was greeted by Hugh – now in civilian clothing and apparently acting as a servant rather than a man-at arms.

"Hello, Hugh," said Wyatt, slapping him on the back. "It is good to see you. How is it with you these days?"

"Welcome, Sir Richard. Well, ah'm nobbut a servant now – except for tax days, that is, when ah'm a man-at-arms again. It's a better life than sittin' on that lookout tower in all weather, ah can tell yer. O' course, there's nowt to look out fer in these peaceful times."

Hugh showed him into a small but well-appointed chamber where Melton was sitting. Melton jumped up with surprise and shook Wyatt's hand vigorously.

"Good to see you, old friend," said Melton.

"And you too," said Wyatt. "But what happened to the gatehouse and palisade that we built? It can't have rotted away. It was only three years ago."

"Ah, yes. Well..." said Melton, awkwardly. "The truth is that the king never did reimburse me for the timber from my woodland, so I sold it bit by bit and built this house with the proceeds – and stones from the castle."

"How is the old the old place?"

"Falling down, I'm sad to say. But you shall see for yourself when you have taken some refreshment – Margery, bring meat and drink!"

Just then, Totty came rushing into the room.

"Ah wanth ter see Thather Thismus!" she lisped.

"Well, Totty," said Melton. "That's not Father Christmas, that's our old friend Sir Thomas."

"But 'ee lookth like Thather Thismus wiv 'is lon' white beard!"

"Not quite white, I hope," said Wyatt, stroking his beard thoughtfully, "though it's true my recent trials and tribulations have put years on me."

Moments later, Mrs Goodlad came into the room with a tray of cold meats and a jug of ale.

"Leave the gen'leman alone, Totty, and go and play in the kitchen – well, if it isn't Mr Wyatt!"

"It's 'Sir Thomas' or 'my lord', to you," corrected Melton. Have you forgotten that he was knighted for his loyal service?"

Wyatt gritted his teeth at that word. At that moment, his loyalty to the king was fragile indeed, for, had it not been for Surrey, would he not still be in that rat-infested dungeon?

"Oh sorry, me lord," said Mrs Goodlad, with a deep courtesy. "Ah forgot all about it – but nobody deserves it as much as you."

"Thank you," said Wyatt.

"Now," said Melton. "Sit down, and I'll bring you up to date with Conisbrough matters."

The affairs of Conisbrough seemed petty to one who had only recently been involved in high affairs of state and played a part in averting the invasion of England, but somehow they seemed more human and more interesting. Wyatt listened with more attention than he had ever paid to the Spanish Ambassador.

"The Castlegardurn men are more trouble than ever. They say that there's no castle to guard now, so why should they pay tax? So once a month, Hugh puts on his old armour, and we go round to collect it. The sight of the armour usually does the trick, though we have had one or two unpleasant incidents."

"What happens then?"

"Hugh claps them in the stocks for a day. Once, poor Hugh was set upon by a gang of thugs. We had to get the garrison of Tickhill to help us. The offenders are still in the dungeon – that's about the only part of the castle that we still use. That reminds me – I forgot to feed them yesterday. Still, serves them right."

"What about Harry and Sally?"

"You remember how the king went back on his word to Aske? It was a terrible time for us all, especially young Harry. A second uprising was begun in Cumberland and Westmoreland, and was spreading to Yorkshire, and I could see that Harry was tempted to join it. Well, it seems that he heeded your words.

He didn't join the rebels, and he stayed loyal to this castle, to you and me, and to the king."

"What is he doing now?"

Melton frowned.

"Well, to be honest, he's got himself into a bit of a mess."

"Tell me about it."

"You know that I apprenticed him to the blacksmith. Well, the blacksmith has a daughter, Susan, and he was planning a cosy little future for them both as man and wife, with Harry taking over the forge, and so on. Trouble is, Harry couldn't get over his fancy for Sally, and to cut a long story short, there was a big fall out over it and Harry was sent away. He's here now, with his sweetheart, but they can't get married because they've got nothing to live on."

Wyatt smiled. It was a matter of grave importance to these people, but he had no doubt that he could settle it easily enough – rather more easily than he had settled Reginald Pole.

"Bring him in."

A moment later, Harry was in front of him, looking rather sheepish.

"So you lost your place?" said Wyatt with a pretence of gravity.

"Yes, sir," said Harry, "but it wasn't because me work was no good, it was..."

Wyatt waved the explanation aside.

"Yes, I've heard all about it. It seems that you were taking my motto too far."

Harry looked puzzled.

"*Loyaulte me lie*. You were loyal to Sally and it cost you your future."

Harry didn't know whether to take this as praise or blame, so he just hung his head and awaited the outcome.

"Well, I commend your loyalty, though I am surprised at it. Higher than you choose their wives for more solid reasons than love – as I did, as my son did – but Sally is a good girl. Where is she?"

It was only a matter of moments before she was standing beside her sweetheart – for had she not been listening at the door?"

"So, young lady, you lured young Harry here from a promising future – but what are you to do now? You can't marry on fresh air!"

Sally had no reply, but a tear trickled down her cheek. Seeing this, Wyatt decided that he had tormented the couple long enough.

"Never mind. Harry's loyalty is to be commended. He resisted the temptation to join the second rising and stayed loyal to the castle and the king – he may have taken loyalty a little too far in matters of the heart, but I am prepared to overlook that. In short, I think I can find him a place at Allington with my farrier. He will have to begin an apprenticeship all over again, but there are good opportunities for a Master Farrier in Kent. What say you, Harry?"

Harry, a radiant smile spreading over his face, said, "Thank you, Sir Thomas. I shall like horse work better than smithying – but..."

"Well?"

"I've heard they're strange folk down south and that the beer is undrinkable."

They all laughed, and Harry hugged his sweetheart. Their little love story was complete – though in saying this so glibly I am guilty of the common error of romantic authors. However, I am not a romantic author, but a writer of historical fiction, so I will correct that comment by stating that the real story of their love had just begun – that difficult road called marriage which has more obstacles than Pilgrim found in his progress to the Heavenly City.

Domestic matters being settled, Melton suggested a tour of the castle.

"You can see from here what happened to the south curtain. Well, you knew what a state it was in. It got worse and worse, with the cracks so big you could nearly walk through them, until one night, last winter, we had a terrible storm. High winds, thunder, lightening – the works. Then there was a clap of thunder louder than any I had ever heard, only it wasn't thunder, it was the south curtain collapsing. It brought the main gatehouse down with it. Soon after that the barbican gatehouse collapsed."

Melton picked up a sack of provisions for the prisoners, and took Wyatt into the bailey, pointing out the range of buildings along the north curtain. "The roofs are full of holes and the water is pouring in. It's not safe to go inside".

Wyatt gave him a concerned look.

"Oh don't worry. I've saved everything I could. Your old chambers are open to the sky now, but I took your lute and your books, and the best of the furniture into my house. It's all in the back room where you'll stay tonight. I saved everything else I could from the buildings, especially the tapestries from the Great Hall, and put them in the storeroom round the back."

He led Wyatt up the steps to the keep. The drawbridge was gone, but had been replaced by some planks of wood. Melton unlocked the door, and immediately a smell of damp and decay hit them. The prisoners in the dungeon heard the door open and sent up a cry for food. Melton walked over to the grating and emptied the bag of loaves he had brought with him.

"What about water?" said Wyatt.

"No need to worry about that. There's a well down there."

He led the way up the winding stair to the Great Chamber. How different it was to when Wyatt had last seen it! The tapestries had gone, put into storage by Melton, and the king's arms had been taken down. The walls were streaming with damp, and the wooden ceiling was rotten and green with mould.

"The roof has gone and the floor of the guardroom has collapsed into the solar. This ceiling will be the next to collapse. We won't go any higher because it's not safe."

"What about the poor devils in the dungeon?"

"Don't worry about them. The dungeon has a stone vaulted ceiling. That won't collapse for another hundred years, if ever. As for this keep, the woodwork might crumble but these walls will stand to the Day of Judgement."

"If stones could speak, just think how many stories this keep could tell," said Wyatt musingly, and that thought seemed to stay in his mind for the rest of the tour and throughout the pleasant meal that they shared together in Melton's house.

Later, in the back room where Melton had quartered him, Wyatt looked out of the small mullioned window that overlooked the castle, mused on the ruins for a while, then picked up a quill, dipped it in ink, and wrote:

*A place of broken bastions, **
Shattered towers and ruined halls;
Time, the mightiest of powers,
Has not spared these ancient walls

No Isabella sits here now
Gazing from her window arch
Over Conisbrough's red rooftops
To distant woods of elm and larch.

No minstrels play the pipe and tabor
Clavicythern, viol or lute,
For all lay in St Peter's churchyard
And all their instruments are mute.

No trumpets clamour in the morning
Proclaiming that the lord will ride
To hunt the hart in Barnsdale forest
Where Robin and his outlaws hide

No lovesick poet scribbles sonnets
To his lover's golden hair;
The halls are empty now and ruined
And only their pale ghosts are there.

No bards of Breton tell their stories
Late into the moonlit night,
Thronged about with raptured listeners

In the cresset's flickering light.

Tales by Wace and Layamon
About this castle they retold:
Of when it was a home to Hengist,
And Arthur in the days of old.

Even the magic power of Merlin
Could not save his lonely cell,
Or all the curious things he treasured
Time was far stronger than his spell.

All, all are gone – though armies failed
To bring about this castle's doom,
Time has too easily succeeded;
And ere long will these bones entomb.

The prophetic soul of the poet! – Three years later Thomas Wyatt died of fever while staying with a friend in Dorset. He is buried in Sherborne Abbey.

NOTE: I searched through all Wyatt's poetry looking for a poem about Conisbrough Castle, but could find nothing, so I filled the gap with a poem of my own. It is nowhere near Wyatt quality, but makes a suitable end to my story.

AFTERWORD

O n the 12th January, 1538, a group of commissioners sent by the king returned the following report on the state of Conisbrough Castle:

Cunesburghe

In primis the yates of the Castelle ffallen downe bothe tymber and stone.

Item the bryge is ffallen downe.

Item one rownde Tower of stone within the seif Castlle of foure storyes height, and the seid Tower wyde within the wales viijth yerdes.

In the loyst storye one welle ffylled vpe wythe gravelle, wiche seid storyes are welle reparyelled but one, wiche seif storye is fallen in decay to the valure of xij towns of tymber and bordes.

Item the decay of leade in the seid Tower to the value of iiij li and more.

Item the wales ffallen downe betwex the seid Tower and the bryge the valew of lx yerdes by estymacon to the valere of cli and more.

Item the stome wales within the Castlee and wales withoute the said Castlle by esymacon to the valewe of cc li and more.

Item to alle reparacons within the Castlle and withoue belongyng to Wright Warke by estimacon to the valewe of viijxx towne and more.

Item their is no artylyrye nor ordynauance within the seid Castelle.

Item no horse mylne their.

Item their remaynthe within the seid Castelle to the valewe of one ffurther and hallfe wich seid leade were of the gotters of the seid Castle.

Thomas Ffairfax.

HISTORICAL NOTE

The main 'character' in my story is Conisbrough Castle in Conisbrough, near Doncaster, South Yorkshire. There has probably been a castle on the same site since Celtic times, but the present stone castle was built in the 12th century and fell into ruin in the mid 16th century. My story is the story of the castle's 'swan song' – its last moment of glory before its final decay.

The poet in my story is Sir Thomas Wyatt (1503–1542), an English ambassador and lyric poet. He is the first great poet of the modern English era, and is credited with introducing the rondeau and the sonnet into English literature. He was born at Allington Castle, near Maidstone in Kent, though his family was originally from Yorkshire. His father, Henry Wyatt, had been one of Henry VII's Privy Councillors, and remained a trusted adviser when Henry VIII came to the throne in 1509. Thomas Wyatt followed his father to court after his education at St John's College, Cambridge. He was rumoured to have had a love affair with Anne Boleyn, which resulted in his imprisonment in the Tower. He survived this to regain the king's favour, was given the Constableship of Kent, knighted, and sent on an important ambassadorial mission to Spain in 1536. He was sent on another mission to France in 1539 on the matter of the king's next wife. On his return, he found himself imprisoned again on suspicion of treason. He died of a fever in 1542 not long after being released from prison.

In my novella I followed Wyatt's life story quite closely, though I made a few small changes for the purposes of my plot. His affair with Anne Boleyn is discussed at length by Schulman, 2011, who explores in detail how far the relationship went, and whether it resulted in sexual relations (see Chapter Five). I decided to emphasise Anne's innocence in this, and all the other affairs she was accused of, in order to add poignancy to my story. Another change was that I omitted Wyatt's ambassadorial mission to France, as my main focus is Conisbrough Castle rather than the Wyatt's biography. I was unable to find Wyatt's motto, but his father's was: *'Oublier ne puis'* (I cannot forget), referring to the time he held out under torture, so I used my old school (Swinton Comprehensive School) motto as it seemed most appropriate: *loyaulte me lie* (loyalty binds me).

Wyatt's father was constable of Conisbrough Castle, and we know from the Conisbrough Court Rolls that he was active in the area. The story of Thomas Drax on pages 7 – 8 is taken from that source and is related in full in Brigdon, 2012. Thomas Wyatt took over the constableship of the castle, jointly with his son, also called Thomas, in 1536, at the time of the Pilgrimage of Grace.

The Pilgrimage of Grace was a popular rising in Yorkshire in October 1536 against Henry VIII's break with the Roman Catholic Church, the Dissolution of the Monasteries and the policies of the King's chief minister, Thomas Cromwell. We know that Tickhill Castle was garissoned with 200 men and artillery (see Brigdon, 2012), and it is a reasonable assumption that Conisbrough was garissoned in the same way, with a similar sized contingent of men-at-arms and artillery. The army of the Pilgrimage, numbering about 40,000 men, met the Duke of Norfolk, with about 5,000 men and artillery, at Doncaster. Negotiations took place and Aske agreed to disperse the army in return for a parliament at York. However, after the army had dispersed, the king went back on his word. The rebel leaders were beheaded, and Aske was carried to York to be hanged in chains. I plead guilty to making a major change to historical events in this part of my story as I describe the pilgrims investing Conisbrough Castle. This never happened, though there can be no doubt that its powerful presence exerted an influence on the events that unfolded at Doncaster, only five miles away.

The dissolution of Roche Abbey is well documented (see Fergusson and Harrison, 2013) and I put into Brother Boniface's mouth some of the words used by contemporaries to describe the pillaging of the abbey buildings. Brother Boniface is a fictional character, as are Harry, Hugh, his wife, Margery, Sally, and Susan. I found the name of Father Ermystead in the list of vicars displayed in Conisbrough Church. It is interesting that he was replaced by William Stansfield in 1537, and I assume that was because he found himself on the wrong side in matters of church and state.

By the end of my story the castle had fallen into serious disrepair. The *Afterword* quotes from a Royal Commission report of 1538, and I took care to ensure that my story matched it in most details. Ironically, it was the collapse of the curtain wall that saved the castle from slighting by Oliver Cromwell. The same report shows Tickhill Castle to be in a similar state of decay, but by the time of the English Civil war it was still defensible, and had to be demolished. This was done so thoroughly that there is not much left today.

Most of the poems quoted in the story are Wyatt's, though I made up the poem written by Anne Boleyn on page 22 (she did write poetry, but nothing relevant has survived), and the poem in the *Epilogue*, as Wyatt wrote nothing about Conisbrough Castle.

BIBLIOGRAPHY

Brigdon, Susan, *Thomas Wyatt: The Heart's Forest*, London, 2012.

Conisbrough Court Rolls, 1304–1347, www.hrionline.ac.uk/conisbrough, accessed May 8, 2017.

Fergusson, P. and Harrison S, *English Heritage Red Guide to Roche Abbey*, London, 2013.

Johnson, Stephen, *Excavations at Conisbrough Castle, 1973–1977. The Yorkshire Archaeological Journal. 52*, 1980.

Marsh, Robert, *An Illustrated Account of Conisbrough*, Conisbrough, 1997.

Oakshott, Ewart, *A Knight and His Castle*, London, 1966.

Oakshott, Ewart, *A Knight in Battle*, London, 1971.

Schulman, Nicola, *Graven With Diamonds, The Many Lives of Thomas Wyatt; Courtier, Poet, Assassin, Spy*, London 2011.

Smith, Henry Eckroyd, *The History of Conisbrough Castle, with Glimpses of Ivanhoe-Land*, Robert White, 1887.

Thompson, M. W., *Conisbrough Castle*, Ministry of Works, 1959.

Did you love *The Poet and the Castle*? Then you should read *Conisbrough Tales* by Christopher Webster!

Conisbrough Tales is a modern version of Chaucer's *Canterbury Tales*, being a collection of stories about my home town, Conisbrough, in verse. I am sure that Geoffrey Chaucer's dog could write better poetry than me, but I think (hope) that there are a few felicitous moments where the doggerel rises to the level of verse (and, at rare moments, perhaps even poetry). Whatever the quality of the writing, I believe that those who know and love Conisbrough as I do will enjoy reading these stories.

About the Author

In Conisbrough, in the West Riding, I spent most of my childhood, where there's an old castle, presiding over the local neighbourhood. The castle teased me with its mystery and got me interested in history. Later, at University, I took a Literature degree, choosing an option on Jane Austen and Regency Society, and also one on poetry: worlds which I loved to get lost in – and now I show appreciation by trying my hand at narration.